THE WARLOCK LEGACY BOOK 9

RYAN ATTARD

Shattered

Ryan Attard

Copyright © 2020 by Ryan Attard. All rights reserved. This is a work of fiction. Any resemblance to actual persons living or dead, businesses, events or locales is purely coincidental. Reproduction in whole or part of this publication without express written consent is strictly prohibited.
Email ryanattardauthor@gmail.com

1

"Amaymon, no! Put the champagne down! Put it dow- Oh, crap. Everyone, *duck*!"

I watched in horror as the demon slid a claw across the half-opened champagne bottle—'sabering' it in his unique way—and bubbly foam that cost way more than I wanted to think about went sailing across my office. Most of it found the wall, the furniture, my desk and computer, but some of it also splattered our party guests.

Which leads us to today's teachable moment: always keep an eye on your demon, especially during festivities.

Despite Amaymon's havoc, this was turning out to be a fairly good shindig, particularly since the person for whom it was thrown—my former apprentice, and current girlfriend, Abi—had not stopped smiling.

This was a long time coming. It was not every day you got to graduate from magical apprenticeship along with nearly a decade of online college.

So, yeah, I threw her a party.

A woman with whom I had lived for nine years, a woman who had stood by me through thick and thin (and there was a lot of thick—or thin, whichever is the bad one). A woman who had still found time to get a college degree, help me kick monster ass whenever the need arose, and who last year confessed her feelings for me.

We've been dating ever since and I have to say, I've never been happier.

"You're smiling at the sandwiches," Amaymon said. I looked up to see him leaning on the kitchen door frame, broken champagne bottle in one hand. "It's getting creepy. Did you piss in them?"

I frowned at him. "What? No, what's wrong with you. I did not piss in the sandwiches."

"Too bad," he said. "That would have been funny."

I sighed. "I'm just preparing some more snacks. Go clean up that mess before someone slips and breaks their neck or something."

"This crowd? Psh! If someone here gets taken down by some bubbly they'll never hear the end of it."

He took a massive swig from the bottle as his eyes travelled over to where Abi was talking to Jack, another former student of mine who had retired from active duty of almost daily mortal danger to pursue the calm and serene life of a blacksmith.

Both of them were giggling over something, while Jack's boyfriend, Luke, surreptitiously glanced over in my direction.

The rest of the partygoers consisted of the Grigori, a group of wizards and specialists that made up the bulk of the magical policing community.

I had only invited the cool ones.

Or, you know, the ones who did not petition to have me tried and executed.

I'm petty like that.

Emrys, an honest-to-god Druid wearing a not-what-you-pictured-when-I-said-'druid' three-piece suit, was telling a dirty joke and not bothering to keep his voice down. Next to him, Evans, a golem eight feet tall and nearly as wide, nodded while scarfing down three sandwiches from the previous tray.

The other two listening in were not Grigori but that did not make them any less powerful.

Turtle was a giant Chinese man with a rotund belly and an equally round shaved head, permanently etched with a Buddha-like smile. He wore his usual forest-green Chinese suit, and carried an oak staff.

Next to him was an angel.

A literal angel.

Yeah. Let that sink in for a moment.

It helped that Anael looked nothing like her winged, majestic self, instead opting for the guise of Doctor Annalise Tompkins, therapist extraordinaire. A pretty, if somewhat mousy, brunette with killer eyes and a heartbreaker smile. She had once been my therapist, before revealing the fact that she had been sent by a rogue faction of angels to spy on me and my friends, while waging a civil war in Heaven.

She had also helped me get my magic back after my depression.

All in all, not a bad egg.

She and Abi had just begun chatting about therapy (Abi had just majored in Psychology) when Amaymon nudged me.

"Who's the angel chick?"

I glanced from him to her and back to him. "Dude, forget it. You have no chance."

Amaymon shot me a look. "That's the one who gave you your mojo back, right? Angel of love."

"Virtue," I said, sighing in surrender. I knew where this was going. "Virtue of Love."

Amaymon wasn't listening. He was already on his way towards Anael, grinning in the exact same way every self-confident jock did before asking out the head cheerleader. I followed along just for giggles, stopping next to Abi and pecking her lightly on the side of the head. She leaned into my chest and we watched the show.

"Hey," Amaymon drawled. He did that alpha-male thing where he placed one arm on the wall, half-trapping her in. "I'm Amaymon. But you've heard of me already."

Anael, to her credit, kept her expression bored and peered at him through her spectacles.

"Hello, Amaymon. Yes, I have heard of you. However, you are currently interrupting the lovely conversation I was having with Abigale. Unless of course you have something to contribute on the subject of behavioral therapy."

"Only when I spray him with a hose while he's in cat form," I interjected.

The glare he shot me contained little more than the promise of feline retribution.

"I've been meaning to catch you," he went on. "You're the angel of love, right?"

She raised an eyebrow. "Virtue of Love."

"Told you," I added.

"And what does that entail?" he asked. "Do you govern *all* forms of love?"

The angel sighed. "Yes," she replied. "All love. Family, friends, straight, gay, sexual, non-sexual—why, even the bond between wizard and familiar. Any and all forms. And yes, that does include lust, which is why you asked that question."

To his credit, Amaymon remained unfazed.

"That's amazing, you must have quite the repertoire. Maybe share one or two tricks with these two," he said, nodding at me and Abi.

"Hey!" she snapped.

"Yeah, hey!" I added. "We're doing just fine, thank you."

"That's your problem, dude," he said. "*Just fine* ain't gonna cut it. I banged many a succubus, including Abi's mom-"

"Please don't remind me," Abi interjected.

"And *fine* don't do the trick anymore," he went on. "Magic chicks need magic sex. You gotta broaden your horizons. Speaking of which..." He turned to Anael and wiggled his eyebrows. "What say you and I break a few universal laws and teach these kids how it's done? For educational purposes, of course."

Anael closed her eyes, exhaled softly and fully turned to the demon.

"Amaymon." Her dulcet tones only conveyed her ire more. "I have never been more repulsed by a single creature in my entire life. Excuse me."

And without another word she pushed past him and walked away.

We all just stood there, stunned, before I—grinning so much my cheeks hurt—pointed at him and started laughing.

"Denied!"

Everyone else joined me in laughing at the demon.

Amaymon glanced after Anael and shrugged. "That ain't a no," he said.

"No, that was a put-down and a verbal castration rolled in one," Abi told him. "Now I have to go apologize to her and keep the only woman in this party from leaving. Where's your sister anyway?"

I shrugged. "I left her a message but no answer. Maybe she got stuck in traffic or something."

Abi raised her eyebrows. Wizards as powerful as my sister don't get stuck in traffic.

"Okay, maybe she's fooling around with Greg," I said. "Payback for the last time *we* were late for dinner."

Abi chuckled at the memory. To be fair, it was a really good memory. She pecked me on the lips and ran after the angel.

I was about to tell Amaymon off for annoying my party guests when my phone rang. I walked to my desk and picked up.

"Erik!" I recognized Greg's panicked tones.

Greg was a Kresnik, sort of an anti-vampire. He was old, he was powerful, and he was a Grigori. Greg and I had been through multiple missions together and the guy was reliable. And, even if he was dating my sister, he was a good guy and I trusted him.

"Erik, she was taken," he spat in a thick Slavic accent that came out even stronger with emotion. "Gil and Mephisto, both were taken by angels."

"What?"

A cold wave rushed through me.

"No time," he said. From the background I heard the sound of a car honking and tires screeching. "They are coming for you next, Erik! I'm on my way."

"What?" I cried. Now everyone was looking at me. "Greg, what's going-"

I heard a sudden pulse of feedback and the phone died. The lights went out half a second later, plunging the office into darkness.

Light flashed from outside.

"Erik." I saw Anael's worried face from across the room. "Erik, they're here."

I ran to the window and watched as angels rained from the sky.

They were like little meteorites with wings and armor, white flashes that took shape and floated around my office, surrounding the building.

A voice boomed loudly in my head with overbearing, otherworldly power.

"Erik Ashendale. Come out and surrender to Heaven's Army. Your time of judgement is now!"

2

The atmosphere changed instantly as we all went into battle mode. Abi and I fell into a well-practiced routine. Vest and body armor for her, coat enchanted with protective sigils for me; she strapped on guns and a single baton of pure gold, I sheathed my magical short-sword Djinn to the small of my back, and a mastodonic pistol on my thigh. The whole thing took about thirty seconds, while the rest of the crowd conjured their own battle armaments.

Emrys bore a cudgel called shillelagh, while Turtle hefted his oaken staff. Luke cracked his neck left and right, and slipped out of his leather jacket. Fumes jettisoned from his shoulders but at least the Pyromancer had the good sense not to light up in my house. Jack's entire body turned gunmetal grey.

Meanwhile, Amaymon rushed to Anael's side, the angel swaying unsteadily. I recognized the backlash of power—something big, mean and powerful was at my doorstep.

"That's Gabriel," she said. She did not reject the demon

as he helped her straighten up. "He's the new commander of Heaven's Army."

"Let me guess," I said. "Michael is still missing."

She nodded.

About a year ago we discovered that the archangel Michael, current leader of Heaven, had disappeared and left his celestial home in chaos. As a result, angels started going haywire and targeting Earth.

Jehudiel, one of the angels I had worked with and who was also an archangel, had splintered into a rogue faction which defended Earth from any unwarranted smiting, but he wasn't about to stop the tide any time soon.

BOOM!

One of the angels had rocketed towards the office, only to be repulsed by my wards. The result was a brilliant mass of metal and feathers, and a lot of yelling from the other angels. I could smell the violence in the air. These guys were out for blood.

"Why are they after me?"

It was Emrys who answered. "Because you have your magic back, Erik," he said.

I could tell he was connecting with the earth. As a Druid, there was very little in terms of limitation to Emrys' power so long as he was connected to the ground.

"You and your sister have more magic than anyone else on the planet," he went on. "You're walking nukes. That doesn't sit well with angels, who are all about balance. And with Gil missing..."

"What?" I snapped. "My sister is missing? Greg said something but he wasn't making any sense."

"My reports show that she stopped answering calls twenty-four hours ago," Evans said, managing to shrug his massive shoulders. "This is not unusual behavior for her, but I just received a report from Greg a few minutes ago indicating that both she and her familiar Mephisto have gone missing."

I grimaced and looked at Amaymon.

Mephisto was his brother, and the two of them were primal Elementals. That made them two of the most powerful beings in existence. If someone could just kidnap them...

Well, it wasn't good.

Not good at all.

BOOM!

Another angel kamikazed himself into my wards and this time I felt the blow in my gut. The whole room shook like a scale seven earthquake.

"Shit," I said.

"Erik," said Turtle. In the midst of panic he was the only calm one. "Perhaps it would be wise to deal with the present issue first, before advancing to the next."

"Right." I strode towards the door. Without prompting, the Grigori fell in line.

"Wait," Anael said.

She spread her arms and her image changed. Now a tall, proud angel took her place, wings whiter than snow spreading, then folding behind her. A two-pronged lance appeared in her hand, matching the gold-and-pearl armor she wore. Auburn hair that radiated cosmic power flowed long and lustrous from her head.

"I shall go first."

She opened the door and took to the air. The rest of us lined on my porch and waited.

Gabriel stood at the forefront of his army. He looked like the lovechild of *Conan the Barbarian* and *Barbie*. Bits of sapphire armor adorned his body, though I noticed that his midriff was bare, exposing chiseled abs that would put Marvel actors to shame. Flaring out behind him were four angel wings, stretching out a good seven feet each. From what little I knew about angel anatomy, the bigger the wings, the stronger the Grace (angelic equivalent to our magical core).

Anael flew up to face him, her two wings stretching twice as long as that. Take that, Goldilocks. Four wings don't mean shit when they're puny.

Gabriel raised his fist when he saw us and a battalion of angels outstretched one hand while drawing back the other. Bows and arrows were conjured out of light.

Oh good, they had infinite ammo and endless weaponry.

"The Fallen Virtue returns," he told Anael.

"Not Fallen, brother," she replied. "Merely allied with a side opposing your regime. But never Fallen."

In response Gabriel reached towards his hip and manifested a golden broadsword that was as wide as my entire face.

"Your actions betray you, Anael."

"Please, Gabriel. My brother, Virtue of Diligence, do not harm these mortals."

Gabriel shot a look at us.

You know when they say looks could kill? Well, that can be literal with angels.

Whatever was up his ass, Gabriel was a Virtue, which made him an archangel in terms of power, which made us very—oh-so-very— screwed.

Magical pressure bore down on us as if someone had turned gravity up by eleven. I felt my shoulders squeeze, my lungs compress, and in the distance I could hear my companions struggle. Anael was saying something but it was distant noise and it didn't matter.

I reached in and grabbed hold of my magic.

Ever since getting my powers back and wrapping up Abi's tutoring, I had been able to devote a lot of time to retraining myself.

Magic, all magic, worked on the same basic principles here on Earth. Angel or not, it was just a matter of scale. But if you know the structure, then you know where the weak points are and you can counter it.

My aura turned black as living shadows wrapped around me. I reached out, feeling the spell that Gabriel had cast on us. Wrapping around the edges of the spell, I began creating a counter-vibration that weakened the spell, reducing its area of effect.

The people on the edges, Abi and Turtle, were the first to be released, then, as the spell narrowed further, one by one everyone got back up. That left only me, who was at the center, taking the whole brunt of it myself. But at this point the spell had weakened and I could push back.

Gabriel cocked his head.

"What else you got?" I challenged.

"Erik Ashendale," he said. "You dare use your filthy, impure magic against our might?"

I shrugged. "Yeah. That's kinda what I do. Don't you guys have memos or something? Also, I know angels can choose their appearance—so why do you have to look like a bodybuilder designed by Richard Simmons?"

Gabriel frowned, his alien mind trying to make sense of my words. Before he could I took out my gun. Everyone else around me did the same, raising weapons.

"Now tell me what you did to my sister," I demanded.

"Gil Ashendale," Gabriel said. "Your sister. We did nothing to her. We could not find her."

"Bullshit," I said, thumbing back the hammer. "That's two outta three, Feather-face."

Gabriel looked at Anael. "Is he insane?"

In response I fired at him. One shot to the chest and Gabriel went down. I had caught him by surprise but the archangel recovered quickly. He spun in the air and careened towards me.

"No!"

Anael dove at him. He parried her spear and the two angels went spinning in mid-air.

The street erupted in battle.

Amaymon roared and threw himself in the air, ripping angels apart no matter how far they flew.

Abi dove for cover and began picking them out one by one. Jack stood next to her, shielding her from light arrows while turning his arms into machine-guns and firing away.

Luke the Pyromancer took to the air and *Human Torch*'ed the whole playground.

Turtle, on the other hand, leaned against his staff and remained very still. I winced. Turtle was a minor god, and we had a deal with a whole group of them. Apparently, they would only actively fight at the right moment, and an angelic militia coming after me was not one of them.

I lunged at Gabriel as he dodged Anael's spear. My magical shortsword, Djinn, flashed azure as I channeled magic into the blade. He parried and we locked blades.

"You wanted me?" I said. "Well, here I am."

I slammed my head into his.

Bad idea.

It was like hitting a concrete wall. Gabriel remained unfazed while I saw stars from one end of the galaxy to the next. He kicked me away and a car broke my fall.

Painfully.

Picking myself out of it, I channeled more magic. Shadows erupted around me and I threw myself in the air. Four angels blocked me but I pushed through them.

"ERIK!"

The monstrous cry was tinted by Greg's Slavic accent.

The one-man cavalry had arrived.

I watched the Kresnik leap from a still-moving car. He swung his cruciform spear at the angels. Light magic met light magic, and the two parties were sent flying in opposite directions. Greg flattened the car he had arrived in.

I tumbled down next to him and helped him up.

"Took your sweet time," I said.

"I found traffic," he said. "Damn tourists."

"Enough!"

It was Emrys that had spoken. His words carried with them a certain degree of authority, but it seemed that there was something else echoing along his words.

I looked down and saw that his shadow did not match his frame. For one thing, his shadow had horns.

Emrys spread his arms and an eerie aura seeped through. I had only sensed that aura once before and that was when an Avatar of God (yes, with the big 'G') had activated his powers.

Emrys was channeling the power of a deity, and not a minor one either.

He looked at Gabriel, who was locked in combat with Anael and frozen on the spot, and said something in a foreign language.

Gaelic, I thought, recognizing some of the softer words.

Emrys finished speaking and switched to plain English.

"Thus spake Cernunnos," he said. "Wilt thou defy the Lord of the Forest?"

Gabriel straightened up. I could tell he was itching to take a swing at Emrys.

"We do not answer to your pagan gods, Druid," he said.

"But you will answer to your Divine One," said Turtle, joining Emrys. "And you will honor the bargain struck, lest the Calamity arises sooner."

Gabriel growled. He looked like he was about to be sick. Finally he lowered his sword, and he took to the air. But not before he turned to give me one final dirty look.

"You will answer to us, Erik Ashendale," he said. "We will correct the imbalance."

I couldn't think of a one-liner and Gabriel wasn't polite enough to wait for one. An instant later, amidst multiple flashes of light, the angels disappeared.

I turned to Emrys. "What the hell is going on?"

The Druid sighed. "Let's go back inside, Erik," he said. "We have much to talk about."

3

We all soberly went back inside. The bunting, drinks and food were present, but the festive atmosphere was gone. The lights were still out—a quick spell from my end created enough ambient illumination to make things comfortable.

The Grigori—Emrys, Evans, and now Greg—all sat on one side. Luke gave Jack a longing look but ended up joining his team as well. Jack looked at the ground.

He knows. Whatever the bad news that was about to follow, he knew.

Same went for Turtle. The big guy just stood in a corner, pouring himself a cup of tea and calmly surveying the room.

Anael had flown off, no doubt rushing to report the situation back to Jehudiel and the rogue angels. Her tone left little doubt about the oncoming conflict with Heaven. The civil war had officially spilled over to our plane.

Abi was nice enough to pour everyone a drink, coffee for most of us, while Amaymon took on his feline form and a black American shorthair curled in one corner of the couch.

No one spoke for a full minute which was the maximum I was willing to wait.

"Someone start talking," I said.

Emrys spoke first. "We have a problem."

I raised my eyebrows. "You think? Let's start simple: what happened to my sister?"

Greg looked away.

"Someone took her and Mephisto," he replied. "It was without a fight. One minute she was in the bathroom changing, the next I heard some voices and Mephisto walked inside to her. There was a flash of light and they disappeared."

"White light?" Abi asked.

He nodded.

"Angels," I said. "They took her."

"We cannot jump to conclusions," Emrys began.

"It's a little too late for that, don't you think?" I snapped. "They already admitted to wanting us."

"They said they didn't have her," Emrys said. "And angels cannot lie."

I shot him a dark look. "Unless they're Fallen."

He shook his head again. "No," he said. "We have been monitoring angelic activity for a while. None of them are Fallen."

"Great," I said. "Just your run-of-the-mill jackasses with cosmic power and an unknown agenda." I realized my hands were hurting—I had curled them into tight fists. "Why come after me?"

It was Turtle who spoke up.

"When you awakened your powers after the Knightmare incident last year," he said, "you unlocked all of your potential. Now you and your sister are two of the most powerful magical entities on this plane. And those powers are tied somehow to the Seven Deadly Sins."

"The Calamity," I said, remembering what they had said outside. "What is that?"

"It depends on who you ask," Emrys said. "For angels, it's the source of all evil and chaos. For a long time we thought it referred to the Demon Emperor but after you... well, you know."

I did know.

A few years ago I had died.

Literally, died. Pull-the-plug, shut-down-all-systems died. I was fighting an evil wizard named Alan Greede, who was also the Sin of Greed. We fought all the way up to a helipad, I rode a dragon (seriously!) and caught up to his chopper, where I got the upper hand until... *something* showed up and chucked me out of the helicopter, while also sealing my healing magic.

The result:

SPLAT!

Concrete, one; Erik, zero.

But it didn't end there. The powers that be—and I had the misfortune to meet a few of them—pulled a few strings, realized that I had plenty more to do in terms of preventing the apocalypse, and so they sent me back...

As a ghost.

This was also during a time when Greede was summoning the Demon Emperor Belial back from slumber, and I piggybacked on the ritual. We both came back to life but only one of us survived the encounter.

What no one told me was that coming back as an angry ghost and getting resurrected would make me the ideal candidate for the Sin of Wrath, which *Jekyll and Hyde*'ed me so bad I ended up fighting my own split personality and losing all of my magic. It was Anael who saw to that, and so here I am now, sane and healthy.

Relatively.

"What's this got to do with Gabriel and his wanting to get to me and Gil?" I asked.

Amaymon chuckled. I looked at him.

"What? It's easy," he said, speaking as if he had figured it out. "They fucked up."

"Who?"

"The morons sitting before you."

I looked at the Grigori.

"We did not," Emrys said. "We... Okay yeah, we fucked up."

"What did you do?"

"Gabriel is a Virtue," Emrys said. "And they only get to full power when it is time for their Sin—their counterpart—to wake up. Both will fight on equal ground leaving only one winner."

"Yeah, I know that," I said. "But there has been no Sin awakening in the past year." I held up my hand and began counting down. "Lust was killed about seven years ago, same with Envy. Greed remains on the run with that asshole. Wrath was destroyed, I'm very sure of *that* one. So that's four out of commission. Leaving behind Gluttony, Sloth and Pride."

"Gabriel's counterpart is Sloth," Abi said. "I did some research on Sins and Virtues. Sloth and Diligence." She frowned at them. "If he's here then that means Sloth has awakened. But we haven't heard of anything."

The Grigori remained silent.

I knew what that meant. Amaymon was right.

Dammit.

"What. The fuck. Did you. DO?" I asked.

"We didn't know," Emrys said. "We didn't know what it was." He sighed. "Okay, enough secrets.

"We don't know when exactly but a couple centuries back, the Grigori of back then discovered a slumbering entity. They did not know what it was because it wasn't anything they had encountered before. It didn't move, it didn't eat, it didn't even sleep. It just sat there.

"So the Grigori decided to use it. They built a Vault to contain it and transported it to—and I quote—'the furthest reaches of civilization'. There they set up a guardian to make sure the entity never awoke, and lined the Vault with a series of siphoning spells that neutralized the entity, as well as took a good chunk of its magical power for them.

"Decades later, a demonologist recognized it as Belphegor. According to him, this was a proto-demon, which had somehow ended up on Earth. Proto-demons have a more malleable DNA. They are constantly evolving, and this one being on a different plane—a weak and relatively nascent one like Earth... Let's just say it messed it up. I mean, this thing doesn't even give off a magical signature. For all intents and purposes, it's dead, except it's not part of that cycle either. It just... *is*."

Emrys paused for a second, giving us time to digest the information he had divulged.

"We don't know how to get rid of it," he said. "So what we do is use Ashendale warlock techniques to siphon its power once every hundred and fifty years."

"Okay," I said. "Then go do it."

"We can't," Greg said. "Not without Gil... or an Ashendale."

"We need you to go to the Ashendale mansion and into the library," Emrys said. "Only one of your bloodline can enter. When we tried, things got... hairy."

I grimaced, thinking of the horrible curses and traps my sadistic forefathers would have left for those who dared attempt to pilfer their precious secrets.

"But that ain't all, is it?" Amaymon asked. "Because you wouldn't all be here just to ask Erik for a library book." He got up and stretched, tail swishing to and fro, before sitting back. "You're here to guard Erik. Because you need him."

Emrys nodded. "The angels have a hit list of three people. Gil is missing, but right now siphoning off Belphegor is more important. Gabriel's presence confirms it."

It clicked.

"Belphegor is the Sin of Sloth," I said. "That's why Gabriel is here."

Emrys nodded.

"About two months ago, one of our scouts reported that Sloth had awakened inside an entity named Belphegor," he said, "which coincides with the timing of the siphoning. If we don't drain the entity's power, the Sin will fully take over."

"Okay then," I said. "Point Gabriel to Belphegor and sit back while the angel works out some anger issues. Problem solved."

"We can't," Emrys said. "We need that power."

A pregnant pause fell in the room.

"You need the power of a Sin?" Abi asked.

"Not the Sin itself, but the host. They are both one and the same now anyway," Emrys said. He shot Turtle a look.

"It's part of our deal with the gods."

Turtle nodded, confirming Emrys' words.

"Why?" I demanded.

"Our reasons are our own. We also wish to be present during the siphoning."

I looked him dead in the eye but he gave me nothing. I knew better than to argue with a deity. I'd learnt that the hard way multiple times.

"You mentioned the angels have a hit list of three people. Presumably three people who can siphon power from Belphegor and the Sin of Sloth," Abi said. "Erik and Gil are two. Who is the third?"

"You will not like this, Erik," Greg said, his voice dripping with disgust.

"Who is it?" I demanded.

Emrys sighed again.

"Alan Greede."

4

"Alan Greede?"
I was practically screaming.
"Alan-fucking-Greede?"

No one stopped me when I balled my fists and stood up. "Where is he?"

Emrys took a while to answer.

"We have him in custody. He surrendered to your sister when she found him less than two days ago wandering the Mojave desert." He raised his glance to meet my eyes. "He was waiting for her."

"Are you sure it's him this time and not some fucking clone?"

He nodded.

"Then let's kill him."

Emrys shook his head. "We can't. Because Greede is the only person who knows how to find Belphegor's Vault, the keys to said Vault, and how to enact the siphoning ritual. He had access to those records. Records that have long since been destroyed." He exhaled loudly. His fists were also balled. "We need him." The words seemed to make him gag.

"No," I spat. "No, I won't work with him. Fuck this, man. And fuck you for thinking I would be game for this."

I sat back down and looked all four Grigori in the eyes one by one.

"This is not how you honor her, dammit."

A chill washed over the room.

Her referred to a former Grigori named Akasha. A woman I had dated for a while. A woman who had been killed (along with several more Grigori members) by Greede while I watched helplessly from a cage.

A death I had yet to avenge.

"That's not fair," Greg said softly.

"It is too fair," I countered. "Greede needs to die. End of discussion."

Turtle cleared his throat.

"You know for whom I speak, Erik," he said gently. "We have foreseen that Alan Greede still has a very important role to play in the upcoming events. As do you."

I sat back down and glared at him. "So let me get this straight: you gods say he's a key player, so regardless of what he might do—like, oh, I don't know, maybe *kill us* for the millionth time—we have to suck it up and play ball. Is that it?"

Turtle said nothing.

"I did not sign anything," I said. "Your deal is with the Grigori. I'm not part of it."

"Do not go down this path, my friend," Turtle said. "You do not need yet another enemy."

I leaned forwards. "Is your sister missing, Turtle? Is Sun Tzu's?"

Before he could reply, Emrys raised his hand placatingly.

"You're right, Erik," he said. "We need to find Gil. She's

our leader and frankly, the most competent one among us. But the fact remains we need the gods on our side. And until we siphon the demon, we also need Greede. After that..." He glanced at Turtle. "You only said you want him at the Vault."

"That is true," Turtle said.

"But you did not say what will happen after."

"Once Alan Greede is physically at the Vault, he will no longer be of interest to us," Turtle said.

"Why?" I demanded. "Why do you need him there?"

Turtle shook his head. "I am not at liberty to say. But I will say this: Greede is not the worst you will face. Prepare yourselves."

He looked up and got to his feet.

"I must leave," he said. "My apologies for the cryptic messages, my friends. Oh, and Abi: congratulations. Your accomplishments are both remarkable and entirely well-deserved."

She blushed. "Thank you."

He gave us one last nod and walked towards the door, disappearing beyond it.

"Well, that was... shitty," Emrys said.

"Could have gone worse," Greg said. "We could have started fighting."

"Not looking forward to that," Evans said, speaking for the first time.

Luke grunted. That was pretty much his entire vocabulary these days.

"Look, Erik," Emrys said. "Until Gil gets back, it falls on me to lead, and hell, I suck at it. Then again, no one else wants the job. It never turns out well—we think there's a curse on it. Regardless, we have to stay on track. Time's running out on Belphegor, especially now that we know he's a Sin and his Virtue is out there looking for him. We need to deal with him ASAP."

"In the meanwhile," Greg said, "I shall keep looking into Gil's disappearance. I have some contacts who might help me trace her."

"I'll help," Evans said.

"Luke and I will keep tabs on any more angel attacks," Jack suggested.

"Don't put yourselves in danger," I told him. "These guys are nothing to mess with."

Jack grinned at me. "Neither are we."

I gave him a nod.

"In the meantime, we need access to the Ashendale library and with Gil missing…" Emrys started.

"I'll make some calls," I said. "Abi, Amaymon, you can take point on that."

Abi nodded. Amaymon yawned.

"Take care of any trouble," I said. "But do not—I repeat, Amaymon: *do not*—harm anyone that doesn't have it coming. Or destroy the house. Or pee in anything." I sighed. "In fact, Abi is in charge of you."

He hissed. "Party pooper," he muttered before going back to sleep.

I ignored him and looked at Emrys.

"Where is Greede?" I asked.

"Locked up," he said. "But, Erik, maybe it's not the best idea for you to come…"

I stood up.

"I'm coming," I said. "That's *my* deal. I'll come to see Greede and tell him exactly who he's messing with."

Emrys stood up too but not in challenge. His shoulders sagged.

"Can you at least promise not to break him?"

"Nope."

He sighed. "Fair enough. Hell, I'm tempted to help you out and call it an accident. But seriously, we need to behave. We need this guy."

I raised my hands.

"I promise I'll be super diplomatic and nice to the homicidal maniac."

"I don't believe you," he said, grabbing his coat. "Anyone else believe him?"

All shook their heads. Abi rolled her eyes.

"What?" I said. "I can be nice. Well, mostly. A little. Okay, fine, *sometimes* I'm nice. Now get your ass out the door and let's go see a man about the end of the world."

5

THWACK!

Alan Greede's head whipped backwards as my fist crashed into his nose. I grabbed the back of his head and slammed it into the table he was shackled to.

"Ow," he moaned through his bloody broken nose.

Emrys sighed. "I thought you were going to be nice."

"He's still alive, isn't he?" I pulled out a chair and sat before the criminal. "Hey, Greede. Long time, no kicking your ass."

Emrys rolled his eyes and took a seat to the side, apparently allowing me to take the lead on this questioning.

Let the diplomacy begin.

Greede cupped his face, blood pouring all over his front. He adjusted his nose with a sickening crack, cried out in agony and looked at me. Black bruises were already forming around his eyes.

"Mr. Ashendale. I have not missed you."

"Ditto, asshole."

Greede craned his head towards Emrys. "And the Druid. Interesting, you being here. I was expecting your sister, Erik.

I do enjoy talking to her. Very civilized. Not to mention easy on the eyes."

"You got a whole lotta face that ain't yet black and blue, Greede," I told him. "Do you really want to keep going there?"

Greede raised his hands.

Well, as much as he could with his hands shackled to the table. Chains rattled as he struggled, but no matter how much noise he made, there was no way in hell they were coming off.

Not unless it was to strangle him with them.

Greede sighed exasperatedly and picked at his sweater. It was the same black sweater he always wore, albeit this one bore the signs of wear and tear. He didn't have his glasses—not that he needed them.

Apart from the new bruises I had given him, he was covered in scratches and scars. Wherever he had run off to in the last two years, he had not been having a good time.

"Fair enough," he said. "Let us attempt some form of diplomacy. How can I help you, gentlemen, today?"

"What do you know about a demon named Belphegor?" Emrys asked.

Greede looked at him. "Belphegor? As in, the current Sin of Sloth?"

"That's the one."

"I would know to run away as far as possible, and hope that it never awakens fully," Greede replied.

"Not good enough, Greede," I said.

"Well it has to be, my dear Erik," he said. "Because when I was still allied with the Sins, that was the one who never attended the meetings, no matter how nice the cookies were. That was the one we all kept hidden and tucked away, never poking it."

"'Was'?" I asked. "As in past tense. Did they kick you out of the club, Greede?"

He cocked an eyebrow. "Do you remember the last time you saw me? The real me?"

"I do," I replied. "I was in a jail cell, incarcerated over a rampage I did not know I had committed, due to a Sin you had implanted in my brain, turning me into Wrath."

He nodded. "And do you know who was with me?"

The image of a stout dwarfish creature, cloaked from head to toe, with a single silver eye gleaming from beneath came to mind.

"Azazel," I said.

"Shut up!" he snapped. Sweat ran through his forehead. "Do not say his name."

"We're forty-five feet underground inside a concrete box lined with some of the best wards known to mankind," I said.

"That's your first mistake," he said. "*Mankind*; he is no man. He's no angel nor demon, either. He's something else." He looked around as if expecting the creature to pop out at the mere mention of him. "He's an *outsider*."

Now it was my turn to shiver.

Outsiders were what we called creatures without any plane of origin. You see, in my world, everyone has a place they came from. Everyone works within a set of rules and laws, and no matter how powerful their magic, there was a logic to everything.

But in between those worlds—or planes, as they are known—lies Chaos space. Emptiness that is not quite so empty. Outsiders are these things that inhabit this space.

"How is that possible?" I asked.

Greede shrugged. "If I knew that, I wouldn't be sitting here. I'd already have won."

"And what would that look like?"

"It's not important. Not anymore." He shook his head. "I lost my Sin after that night. Azazel would have taken it back, and my life along with it, had I not foreseen to my safety. I cast Mammon out of my body and I stand before you now as a common wizard."

I glanced at Emrys. He nodded, confirming Greede's story.

"How is it you exorcised the Sin from yourself? It's supposed to bind to your soul," I said.

He grinned. "I am a very, very smart cookie, Erik. I figured it out. But the method will solely apply to me, given that I know myself and also know how and where to modify my own composition in order to expose flaws in the link between myself and Mammon to sever. Should I attempt this on anyone else, they are more likely to die."

"So to summarize," I said, "you're depowered, a pain in our ass, and also hunted down by the same things that are chasing me."

Greede cocked his head. "It seems that you need me for something." He looked at Emrys. "Related to Belphegor no doubt."

Emrys nodded. "We need you to find the Vault."

Greede stared at him for a long moment. Then he threw his head back and laughed.

"What's so funny?" I demanded.

"Oh, nothing," Greede said, wiping away a tear. "It's just... you are all so hopeless."

"Start making sense, Greede," I growled.

"You want to siphon Belphegor," he said. "But it's too late now. Azazel imbued him with the Sin of Sloth, and over the last couple of centuries, it's been slowly rousing him from his millennia-long slumber. You can't contain the power now."

He paused, frowning in thought.

"But you *can* destroy it, provided you have the right tools."

"Our ancestors siphoned magic from Belphegor," Emrys insisted. "And we will do the same."

"Then ask his sister," he said, looking at me. "She's the smart one. She'll agree with me."

"We can't," Emrys said, through gritted teeth. "She's... indisposed."

Greede frowned at him. "What's happened to her?"

"Why do you want to know?" I shot at him.

"Because she's the one with enough brain power to figure out how to destroy that Sin without it going nuclear," Greede replied. "She and I can lead a ritual to depower it."

"Why are you so eager to help?" I asked.

"Because now that Azazel has turned against me, I want to see him fail," he replied simply. "Fret not, I am not on your side, Erik. But neither was I ever on his side either. I am on *my* side. And right now it is more profitable to help you than it is not. Now, what happened to Gil Ashendale?"

"We don't know," Emrys admitted. "Best we can tell, angels took her."

Greede glared at us for a moment. Then, in a display of rare anger, he slammed his fist down hard on the table.

"*Stupid!*" he exclaimed. "You heroes can be so blind. How could you not foresee that this could happen? Gil Ashendale is a threat, not because of her power but because of her mind. She was the most vulnerable against such an event and you allowed it to happen."

He huffed.

"With her gone we are very limited in what we can do,"

he said, back in his usual tone. "But it's not impossible. We'll just have to take the scenic route."

"What are you talking about?" I asked.

Greede smiled. "Oh no. No more information about the Vault or anything else. Not until we discuss my release."

"Your release?" I echoed. "How about I *don't* throw you off a helicopter and we'll consider us square?"

He chuckled. "No, sorry. I'm not going to sit and rot here while also helping you prevent yet another apocalypse."

"One you didn't set up, anyway," I shot back.

"Which is why you need me," he said. Then he turned to Emrys. "Now then, I'm ready to hear your offer."

The Druid eyed him for a long second. I could practically see the wheels turning inside his mind.

"A full stay of execution, and you spend the rest of your days in a comfortable stronghold with no outside communication. That is the best I can offer under the charges brought up against you."

"Wait, what?" I practically screamed. "He gets to lounge in some fucking resort?"

"Hardly," Emrys said. "It's a stronghold. Maximum security inside a pocket dimension. We will regulate everything coming in and out of there."

I opened my mouth to speak but no words came out. This was fucking bullshit! That guy deserved to be flayed alive and thrown into an acid pit, not to live out his life in a quiet place doing some reading.

"What about my restrictions as I accompany you?" Greede asked.

We both looked at him.

"What? You didn't think I was going to sit this one out, did you?" he asked.

"If you think we're going to let you come-" I began.

"Very well," he said. "Good luck hunting clues."

He folded his arms.

"I can beat it out of you," I said.

He grinned. "Go ahead. But how will you verify that my information is correct? And on such a time-sensitive issue too."

I looked at Emrys. He had been right when he said he was not leader material because I could sense him about to cave.

"Very well," he told Greede. "You will be accompanied by Erik and myself, and you will wear a power dampener at all times. No magic under any circumstances."

I growled inwards and resisted the urge to toss Emrys a few choice words.

"At least let me use magic to defend myself," Greede countered.

"You won't need magic so long as you adhere to your escort."

Greede paused to consider for a moment. "Very well, I accept your terms. I'll reveal our plan of action once I am out of this cell and outside. Preferably eating a burger. I have missed those."

Emrys didn't say anything. He just stood up and walked out, leaving me alone with Greede. He was beaming at me.

He knew he had won this round.

Feeling bile rising in my stomach, I walked out after the Druid.

"Are you kidding me?" I said, catching up to Emrys outside Greede's cell.

"What was I supposed to do?" Emrys snapped back. "He

has us by the balls. But with the restrictions he won't be too much trouble."

"This is Greede we're talking about," I said. "He will find a way to screw us. He always does."

Emrys grinned, shedding what I now realized was a mask of incompetence, and revealing a wolf beneath.

"Let him try," he said. "I have sanctioned the use of lethal force if he so much as sneezes in the wrong direction."

"You want him to fuck up, so you can kill him," I said, finally understanding.

"Of course," he replied. "But not before he gives us what we need. Then we tempt him, and when he steps out of line, we kill him. End of story."

"You're planning on double-crossing a master double-crosser," I warned. "No matter what you have up your sleeve, you can rest assured he will have twice as many schemes."

"Erik," Emrys said, "we know. And trust me, we're ready for anything. And so long as you're there, you can keep him in check until the time is right. What do you say?"

What could I say? On one hand, Greede being killed would be perfect. But on the other, this felt scummy and underhanded. It felt political, almost. Then again, it wasn't my play. And if this is what I had to do in order to get Gil back, then so be it.

I nodded at Emrys.

6

The burger joint wasn't too noisy but we still picked a table that was secluded from the casual hubbub of the popular fast-food chain. We chose a table, not a booth. Have you ever tried to quickly move inside one of those things? It's a nightmare.

Emrys and I sat on either side of Greede. I ended up doing the ordering at the counter because there was no way Greede was going to get up by himself, while Emrys wasn't too familiar with fast-food chains.

I returned with burgers, fries, nuggets, and drinks for the whole table. Greede picked a double-patty and went to town on it. I did the same and finished before him, and thus claimed the last one.

Look, I know it's childish but boys will be boys, and everyone knows men are dumb sometimes. Just leave us to our testosterone-fueled petty competitions and try not to judge us too harshly. We're simple creatures.

I also had another reason for eating a lot: magic. With my level of power and the kind of energy I'm moving around on a daily basis I need my calories. Spell-work is taxing on the body and if I failed to adequately maintain my physical health it was at my own peril.

"And to think I spent all those years dieting and hiring professional nutritionists," Greede said, sighing contentedly.

I munched on a fry and sipped my soda.

"You've eaten," I said. "Now start talking."

He grinned. "Can I get dessert first?"

"Sure," I said. "But how will you enjoy it with no teeth?"

Greede shrugged. "I could get a milkshake."

"Enough," Emrys snapped. He bore his eyes into Greede. "The Vault. Tell us what we need to know, or you're going back into the smallest, darkest hole I can find."

Greede exhaled theatrically. "Very well then." He set down his soda and picked out three straws.

"Think of the Vault as a prison. What do all prisons need? A key. Or keys, in this case. Plural. And these aren't any regular keys either. Something like Belphegor needs special locks and that means very special keys. Are you with me so far?"

I looked at Emrys. "Can I punch him for being condescending?"

The Druid ignored me. Guess one of us had to be the grown-up.

"What can you tell us about these keys?" he asked.

"That they are ancient, powerful, and belong to the gods," Greede replied. "There are three." He placed one straw down. "The Spear of the Sun, formerly belonging to the Celtic god Lugh. Now lost through the ages."

He set a second straw on the table. "The Aegis shield of Zeus. Last I heard it was still in his possession."

"And finally—" He laid down the final straw "—the Holy Sword."

"Excalibur?" I asked.

Greede rolled his eyes at me. "Its prototype. Excalibur, originally known as Caliburn, was a copy of the original Holy Sword. That one is still tucked safely away from prying hands."

"So we need three magical artifacts that belong to gods," I summarized.

Suddenly the burgers didn't sit so well in my stomach.

What Greede was describing was as close to impossible as you could get. See, you can't just sidle up to a god and *ask* to borrow his special toy. Weapons like that become part of the deity's identity. Removing them would be akin to cutting off a limb.

Not only that, but the specific gods he had mentioned were bad news. If you struck down Zeus—through whichever Hail Mary you managed—then you brought down on you the wrath of the Greek, Roman, and possibly Egyptian pantheons. I had dealt with two gods from those—Bacchus and Ceres—before, and even those idiots were a big deal.

If they decided to go to war—forget it. We might as well just make our peace now.

And then there was Lugh. I don't know much about Celtic mythology, but I do know they are some of the most influential and powerful gods around. They are powerful enough to be intrinsically tied to the flow of magic on this plane. They could theoretically make it impossible for us to use magic, permanently crippling us.

Emrys stood up.

"Excuse me," he said, taking out his cell phone. He walked away and began chatting rapidly in Celtic. It made sense. He had spoken it before and besides, Druids are Celtic.

Moments later he switched to Mandarin Chinese.

Greede interlocked his fingers and watched him with amusement. I observed the both of them, once again feeling like there was a game being played beneath the surface that I was missing.

Emrys sat down minutes later.

"The Aegis has been secured, provided it would be loaned on the spot," he explained. "It will be provided at the location of the Vault."

I frowned at him. "Just like that? What, you have Zeus on speed-dial?"

He grinned and said nothing.

Well, color me impressed. Emrys might not have known how to negotiate with prisoners but he sure as hell knew how to make good contacts.

"Well, that's one down," I said. "Two more to go."

"Actually just one," Emrys corrected me. "I have a contact who will lead me to the Spear. It is something I have been looking into for a while now, and it is high time that effort paid off. So, all we need now is to find the Holy Sword. Greede, where is it?"

"Heaven," he said.

I nearly choked on the last of my soda. "What?"

"Heaven," he repeated. "The Holy Sword goes by another name: the Sword of Michael." He chuckled. "So all we have to do is get to Heaven, sneak into the lost archangel's private armory, and we're in business. Now, how about that milkshake?"

7

Okay. Let's recap so far:

I had been forced to work with my nemesis trying to locate a mysterious Vault containing a super-powerful demon for which we needed three magical keys slash godly weapons.

My partner, a Druid and now the Grigori's de facto leader, had managed to secure two out of three with just one phone call (the best I can do with one phone call is takeout and even that comes out wrong sometimes).

Which left us with finding and somehow stealing the Sword of the archangel Michael, who was not only the leader of Heaven, but was also missing.

Oh, and lest I forget, said heavenly forces were after me, my sister, and the aforementioned nemesis.

I'll have 'clusterfuck' for two hundred please, Alex.

So, left with no other option, I took us, plus Amaymon for extra security, to the only place I could think of to help us:

Therapy.

. . .

Doctor Annalise Tompkins' office was white, with very sparse decorations. The air conditioning unit kept the room at a crisp, comfortable temperature, while an air purifier occasionally puffed out bouts of perfumed air. It stood right next to a ficus that had grown very well since the last time I had been here. A pale blue plastic spray bottle sat next to it.

The four of us were lined up before her chair: myself and Emrys on the couch, Greede on a smaller version of her chair, and Amaymon sitting on the edge of a small decorative table. If she minded, the angel said nothing.

Anael sat before us in a black, high-backed chair, wearing a white blouse and black trousers, along with modest heels, and minimal make-up. On this occasion her hair was shoulder-length and wavy. Her spectacles were black-rimmed without being hipster, and her lips were thin and smiling.

Only her eyes, glowing with iridescent power, betrayed her true nature.

"Well," she began. "This certainly is an interesting line-up." She turned to me. "It's nice to see you in my office again, Erik. You seem to be doing well."

I nodded. "As well as I can be, given the circumstances."

"Nonsense," she said. "Like I keep telling you, circumstances have no power over us. They may present a problem but it is up to us to decide how to handle them. *That* falls on our shoulders." She smiled, making my stomach flutter. "You seem happy."

"I am," I said, thinking of Abi and my magic, and all the progress I had made since my trauma.

Anael glanced at Amaymon, who was grinning at her.

"Amaymon," she said politely. "Nice to see you again. I don't suppose you're here to book an appointment."

He chuckled. I glared at him.

"Oh, come on, she practically fed me that one," he said. "Besides, I would love to see you again."

"I'm sure you would," she replied neutrally. "But I'm afraid you'd be disappointed."

"Have more faith in yourself, babe," he shot back. "I'm sure you'll be able to keep up." He leaned forward. "Hey, did you come up with your name? Because if you take Anael and shave off a vowel, you end up with something very popular-"

"Amaymon!" I snapped.

To her credit Anael chuckled. She might be the only angel with a sense of humor.

"You sad creature," she said, pityingly. "You've never known love, have you? And now that you have, you know not what to do with your feelings."

Amaymon scowled at her.

"Gay," he said. And with a shrug he turned into a cat and curled upon himself.

I looked at the angel apologetically. Anael just kept on talking.

"And welcome, Druid," she told Emrys. "I see you brought the enemy along with you."

Greede nodded at her. "Pleasure to meet you. I understand you are an angel."

"My name is Anael, archangel and Virtue of Love," she replied.

"Never heard of you."

"No," she said. "*You* certainly would have never heard of me. But I have heard of you, Alan Greede." Her eyes flashed with power, the glare caught by the spectacles and reflected off.

Just for a second I entertained the possibility of Anael smiting Greede where he stood but no such luck.

"We need some help," Emrys said.

And he proceeded to tell her all about Sloth and the Vault. Anael sat there, taking it all in, nodding at intervals but otherwise remaining statuesque.

When Emrys finished his tale, she turned to Greede.

"I will hear your version of events now," she told him.

He beamed at her. "I'm an open book."

"Where is your Sin? I do not sense it."

"I cast it off," he replied. "After the Knightmare incident, I was forced to reconcile myself to the fact I could no longer depend on my patron."

Anael nodded in understanding.

"Since all the Sins were created by his power," Greede went on, "my power linked me to him. Which left me with all the liability of having a demonic spirit inside of me without any of the advantages. So I extricated it."

"Is that even possible?" Emrys directed towards Anael. "I've never heard of it happening."

The angel nodded. "He does not lie."

"I am mortal," Greede said. "He thought that leaving me powerless without his Sin would make me weak but he did not know that I am a survivor. I am strongest when I am just human."

All of us stared at him.

It much was true. Greede's power wasn't his magic. It was his ability to survive anything, manipulating circumstances to his advantage. That's purely a human skill and he had mastered it to an artful degree.

Anael cocked her head.

"That is the most truthful you have been in the last three hundred years," she said.

"Three hundred years?" I echoed. "Just how old are you, Greede?"

He shrugged. "Who knows anymore?"

"Our records indicate his presence at the time of Babylon," Emrys said.

I was sure my jaw had slackened.

Babylon—no wonder the guy was powerful. He was older than most religions!

With a deep breath I filed that information away and focused on the task at hand.

Anael was looking at me.

"Will you help us?" I asked.

"Tell me what you need," she said.

"Do you know where Michael is?"

She burst out laughing. "If I, or any angel, knew that, we wouldn't be in this mess," she said. "Be it Gabriel or Jehudiel, both sides want our true leader back. Unfortunately, he disappeared about three years ago."

I swore. She gave me a reproachful look.

"Sorry," I said. "But we're screwed then. Without the Sword of Michael we only have two out of three."

Anael cocked her head. "The Sword? You did not specify that you *only* require the Sword. You asked the wrong question. This is why I gave you the wrong answer."

"What?"

Greede had apparently caught on. "When Michael disappeared, he didn't take the Sword with him," he said. "Which means he didn't go to war." His eyes widened. "Oh, I see now."

"What do you see?" I asked.

"Ask the pretty angel," he said, looking at Anael. "Ask her why Michael is gone. And why her faction of rebels has readily sided with the Grigori, defying the golden rule of celestials."

"Do not take sides," Anael said. She removed her spectacles and pretended to clean them. "But we did. Jehudiel was branded a heretic for it. And we did so because of Michael."

She put the glasses back on.

"When you died, Erik," she began, "you mentioned a creature that pushed you out of Greede's helicopter."

I shot Greede a look. He seemed very keen on the painting on the wall.

"That creature is what we refer to as the Calamity," she said.

"What is it?" I asked, turning to Greede.

He remained silent.

Amaymon made a single hissing sound that sent a wave of terror coursing through me. This was just the aftershock —Greede paled and his right hand began shaking involuntarily.

"He asked you a question, flesh bag," the cat drawled. He never raised his head.

"I do not know," Greede admitted. "I do know that... thing... is not human. And it was a Sin long before any of us. Long before Lilith too. It's the first Sin."

Anael closed her eyes.

"And it was this creature's presence that forced Michael to his pilgrimage," she said.

"Pilgrimage?" Emrys asked. "For what? And more importantly, when will he return?"

Anael looked at him. "When he finishes."

Apparently Emrys understood the meaning behind her terse words better than I did because he nodded.

"We still need to get into Heaven," he said. "And to... um, borrow... the Holy Sword."

Anael smiled. "You mean to steal from the most powerful angel that ever existed, a being whose creation birthed the universe as a side effect?"

The Druid shrugged. "We all must do what we must." He reached into his suit jacket pocket and pulled out what looked like a dried leaf. He handed it over to Anael, who took it reverently and stared at it.

Then she smiled.

"So I see." She handed him the leaf back. "How is old Cernunnos faring these days?" she asked conversationally.

"Eh," Emrys replied. "Still grumpy. At least in this century he gets to smoke weed and hook up with co-eds on Earth Day."

Anael chuckled.

I tried not to drop my jaw again.

Cernunnos. The god of nature. The being literally in charge of every inch of soil, root, and leaf around us. The guy who could call Mother Nature his daughter.

And Emrys was on speaking terms with him. Now that phone call started making sense.

Talk about friends in high places.

"Very well," Anael said. She stood up, went to a filing cabinet and returned with a laminated key card.

She handed it to me.

"That will get you through the pathway."

I grinned. "Don't you mean stairway?"

She looked at me blankly.

"You know, cause of the song? *Stairway to Heaven*," I said. "It goes *Stairway to Heaven*, and *Highway to Hell*."

"We have an elevator," she replied plainly, clearly missing the joke.

Emrys shook his head. "And they say I'm terrible with puns."

"You don't gotta live with him," Amaymon interjected.

"You're both dead inside," I retorted.

"The card will get you through to Heaven," Anael said,

"but you still have to find a way-station. A portal that links Earth to Heaven. And those will be heavily fortified by Gabriel's forces."

Great.

Out of the frying pan, and into the mob of smiting celestial bodies with a grudge against me.

But Anael was still grinning.

"Fortunately for you, I have the perfect distraction."

8

The Ashendale Mansion, usually a bastion of law and order, was now a chaotic hustle and bustle of maids and other members of staff running amok with boxes and crates, while soldiers patrolled the corridors and doorways, checking the identification of everyone who entered.

Above the entropy, Abi's voice could be heard giving out orders, directing the flow like a scout to a beehive. She paused when she saw me entering along with Greede and the Grigori, and marched towards us.

She gave Greede a dirty look.

Then punched him in the face.

"Why is he here?"

Greede pressed his now twice-broken nose, and groaned. I chuckled.

"Long story," I told her. "Basically, we have to get in bed with him."

"Ew."

"Sorry. Phrasing. But we have to play nice. For now. Or until he pisses us off."

Abi shot Greede one final look and dragged me aside.

"It's chaos here," she told me. "The staff is disordered without Mephisto to direct them. Apparently, he kept them in separate wings and never fully divulge what the whole mansion's duties are."

"Divide and conquer," I noted. "Yeah, that's Mephisto alright."

"Well, it's a goddamn tornado," she said. "And how many libraries does Gil need? I've been at it this entire time and still nothing. Oh, and we found a chest."

I raised my eyebrows. "Come again?"

"A locked magical chest, full of books. It's where Gil hid all the important stuff." She looked at me like I was slow. "Did you forget you were supposed to use whatever bloodline magic you have to give us access to material about the siphoning ritual?"

She huffed out a breath and pulled me towards a big, red pirate treasure chest-looking piece of furniture. It had no lock but the front was bolted shut, the locking mechanism melded with the seams.

"I was expecting a secret wall in the library," I commented as I knelt by it and drew Djinn just enough to cut my finger. Before my automatic healing magic kicked in, I smeared some blood on the chest and the mechanism clicked.

"I guess your sister likes pirates," Abi commented. "It's certainly more portable than a secret door in the library."

"Yeah, but that would have been so cool."

She rolled her eyes. "You would really love a lair, wouldn't you?"

"I already have a lair," I said. "It's the castle on top that I can't afford."

Dull clanging echoed, and the chest popped open.

The inside was empty.

"What the crap..." Abi knelt beside the chest and felt around. "Nothing. No false bottom or anything."

I signaled Emrys over. "We have a problem," I said, indicating the chest.

Then it was the Druid's turn to swear.

"Without that ritual we are screwed."

"Not entirely," came Greede's drawl from the background.

He had been made to sit on the side, with two soldiers flanking him and his hands cuffed in front.

"We could just destroy the Sin," he suggested. "Provided you're willing to make the commitment."

"What commitment?" Emrys asked.

Greede's grin was reptilian.

"The worst one. The commitment to let go of a massive source of power, possibly leaving yourselves vulnerable and losing the fight." He leaned back. "But then again, it's not like you can afford to destroy something like that, can you? I mean, look at what remains of the great Grigori."

He gestured to the side, where the rest of them were busy coordinating our next plan of attack.

Mustafa, the Abjurer with a turban and a bushy mustache; Luke the Pyromancer; Greg, leaning on his spear, telling everyone he will not be joining them. Apparently, he had a lead on where Gil could be and was following it. Evans, the golem, nodding his comically small head. With them was also a humanoid, gelatinous blob wearing a yellow raincoat and a baseball cap. That would be Seneschal, the Slime.

Yep, an actual living, sentient slime, who was also an accomplished Biomancer—whatever the heck that was—and polymorph.

"Oh, how the mighty have fallen," Greede said. "Shame. It all went to hell the moment your leader abandoned you. And I don't mean the pretty Warlock lady." His eyes narrowed. "Your First Seat."

I never saw Emrys move. One minute he was next to me, the next a massive brown bear was swatting Greede off his chair and on the ground, while everyone looked on. Greede tried crawling away. I could feel energy around him as he tried to call up his power, but the cuff stunted the magic.

The bear stepped on him, and Emrys turned human, his foot planted on Greede's neck.

"What do you know of our first?"

Let me explain:

You see, the Grigori have a ranking system, one through ten. Gil occupied the second seat, which made her the leader. That's because the first seat, the highest-ranking member of the Grigori, had disappeared decades ago. Don't ask me why they were never replaced—maybe the seat was cursed, or maybe whoever occupied the seat was known for taking long hiatuses.

Either way, it was clearly a touchy subject.

"They left," Greede wheezed as Emrys' shoe crushed his throat. "That, and rumors." He managed a laugh. "Of how weak you've become."

Emrys reached down and with superhuman strength picked him up by his sweater.

"I'm too exhausted to listen to your bullshit," he said, tossing Greede back into the chair. The latter cracked his head against the wall. "We have a real problem here and now. If you have a solution, talk. But one more jibe and I will slit your throat and throw your corpse to the wolves."

I was pretty sure he was being literal with the wolf part.

Greede rubbed his neck.

"Fine. We're getting three of the most powerful weapons in the universe, plus a team of highly trained individuals to wield them. Not everyone can just carry something of that power. You need to be worthy. And that usually means possessing a certain affinity towards the weapon. If we can carry the weapons, then we can use them, too," he said. "So I say, instead of siphoning off Belphegor, we plunge the Sword of Michael through his heart, and be done with it once and for all."

"Thus robbing Azazel of another Sin," Emrys concluded. He turned to the other Grigori. "What do you say?"

"We've managed thus far without the demon's power," Evans said. "I am sure we can keep doing so, as long as we remain united."

"We kill demons," Greg said simply. "I say aye."

"I concur," Mustafa said. "The Vault itself is a trove, but the demon is more trouble than it is worth."

Luke grunted his approval. Seneschal's blobby face stretched until a smile appeared, and he fist-pumped in the air.

Guess that's Slime for "Hell yeah!"

"Erik," Emrys said, turning to me, "it seems you are going to get what you want after all. The Sin of Sloth will be destroyed."

I nodded and saw Greede smiling in approval.

Funny, I was just thinking he was also getting what *he* wanted.

I PULLED Abi aside while everyone else was having lunch. We found a study and I closed the door behind us.

Leaning in, I kissed her.

"Woah," she said, when we parted. "What brought this on?"

I grinned. "Went to therapy. She kinda reminded me of what really makes me happy."

Abi raised an eyebrow. "The really hot angel made you horny?"

I kissed her again. "No, my really awesome girlfriend did. Besides, I'm too naughty for an angel."

She laughed but I know her. I know when something's bothering her.

"What?" I asked.

She sighed. "It's silly."

"Let me be the judge of that."

She exhaled. "I'm no longer the apprentice," she said. I nodded. "So what am I?"

"Um..." Okay, now I was getting confused. "My girlfriend?"

"Erik, you know what I can do to people's minds," she said. "How can I be certain that our feelings for each other are genuine, and not a byproduct of... you know... my succubus powers?"

"They don't work on me," I told her.

She raised her eyebrows. "No, you have a higher tolerance, not complete immunity. But we've been living together for almost a decade. Maybe enough to change things subtly. Like a slow poison."

"Okay, let me stop you right there," I said. "Stop referring to this as poison. Or anything negative. That's unfair."

I took her hands.

"It's unfair to everything we've been through. It's unfair to the struggles we went through to get to this point," I told her. "Abi, I love you. And you know what it takes for me to say that."

She nodded. "I told you it was silly. And I love you, too."

This time she kissed me.

"Crazy life we live, isn't it?" I said. We both chuckled. "Look, I have to go. I have to end this."

"I'll come with you," she said. "No point in me staying here-"

"No," I said, perhaps a bit too harshly. "No, Abi, I'm sorry, not on this one."

She stepped back. "Oh come on, are you seriously sidelining me?"

I shook my head. "No, I'm not. But we need to play to our strengths."

"Like I can't handle myself in the field," she retorted.

There was a time when that was true. But not anymore. Remember how I died? Well, turns out I had been gone for a year, and left my town unprotected against creatures. Abi had taken up the slack, punching far above her weight class, and nearly getting killed. She didn't have my power or my healing.

Yet she stepped up.

"You can," I said. "Hell, you might be better at it than half the people my sister trains. But this is a celestial-level battle. We're talking raw power here. And that's me."

She crossed her arms and pursed her lips the way she did when she knew I had outmaneuvered her.

It happened.

Very rarely.

"I want you to help Greg," I told her. "But behind the scenes. And I want you keep tabs on the Grigori."

Abi cocked her head. "Why?"

"Because something stinks like a Greede scheme," I said. "Think about it: first he gets out, then he worms his way into working with us... he's going to screw us over, it's just a matter of when. But now there are these artifacts involved. Greede doesn't have the power for them, not anymore, but the Grigori do."

"And if one of them was in bed with Greede..." she carried on.

I grinned. "Ew," I said, imitating her.

She raised her eyebrows. "You think you're so funny."

"I have my moments."

She rolled her eyes. "Fine, I'll stay here and play secretary."

"I'd rather you play spy," I told her. "But Black Widow, not James Bond."

"I'm not wearing the costume, Erik."

"It was on sale and you looked great in it for Halloween," I argued.

"Damn right I did," she said. Despite herself she grinned. "Okay, I'll find your sister. And I'll keep watch. Just do me one favor."

"Anything."

"Take Amaymon with you," she said.

I raised my eyebrows quizzically.

"Maids?"

"Ten complaints this month. And sadly, it's been a slow month."

I rolled my eyes. "Fucking cat. I'll take him off your hands."

"Take him off the edge of a cliff," she said. "A high one. With spikes at the bottom."

"Yes, dear," I said, before kissing her and leaving again.

9

The rendezvous point was a field in the middle of nowhere, until the teen angel showed up. Seriously, he looked like a tenth-grader in LARP cosplay, with freckles on his face, awkwardly running in his armor.

He located Emrys and beamed at him.

"All here? Good. Hold hands, please."

All of us looked awkwardly at one another before Amaymon snatched my hand and grinned. I rolled my eyes. I took Greg's offered hand, as the rest of the Grigori and Greede locked hands with the angelic page boy.

One flash of light later and we were at a military camp of sorts, with white being the dominant color instead of green.

Angels, all haggard and bearing the signs of injury, along with battered armor and chipped weapons, prepared their armament. Celestial beings or not, I recognized the grim look in their eyes: the look of someone ready for one last stand.

"Erik Ashendale."

A small supernova announced his arrival. Jehudiel looked...

Older.

He was still over six feet tall, but his massive SUV-sized wingspan had been reduced. Once lustrous hair was now grey and long, frazzled and frayed at the ends. His armor was still golden and solid, but it was now marred with dark spots.

His eyes, cosmic black holes of untold power, looked tired and at the end of the line.

"Jehudiel," I said. "You... well, you've looked better."

The archangel shook my hand and gave the others a cursory nod.

"Welcome to what is left of the rogue angelic army," he said. "Please have a seat and make yourselves comfortable. We will begin our briefing shortly. Erik Ashendale, I will speak with you."

Without waiting for a response, he walked off to the side, expecting me to follow. I did.

"I heard what occurred to your sister and her demon familiar," he said. "Worry not, this is the will of our leader."

"Michael," I said. "You think he's got her?"

Jehudiel nodded. "I have my suspicions, yes."

"Why?"

"Because you and your sister have now become the most dangerous, powerful mortals in the plane," he said. "You have untold power. Enough to tip the scales. I suspect Michael has known this for some time now and has taken measures to protect your sister."

"While I get stuck with the Scooby Gang," I added.

Jehudiel smiled. "You were always averse to bowing out of a situation, even at great peril to yourself, if memory serves."

I rolled my eyes. "Touché."

We walked a little further towards the edge of the camp.

"There is news," Jehudiel said. "About Gabriel."

"What about him?"

"He too has disappeared," he said. "The Virtue of Temperance came into power about six months ago, while the angel in question was away. My sources tell me he disappeared only to return a few days later."

Wheels started turning in my head. "You think there's foul play afoot?"

Jehudiel grinned. There was a time he would not have gotten my word play.

"Yes," he said. "And when he returned with his new power, Gabriel announced his plans for invasion. Starting with building way-stations between Heaven and this plane, thus allowing the angels who are shunted here to still maintain contact with their original source. Thus far only one has been completed."

I nodded.

That's the thing with higher beings: Earth is too small for them. They have to maintain a connection to their home base or risk withering away. I had actually used that loophole once to defeat a Fallen Angel, an archangel called Raphael.

"Wait," I said. "How are your people surviving? Do you have a way-station too?"

Jehudiel shook his head.

And then it dawned on me. *He* had been feeding his people his own Grace. That's why he looked so haggard and weak.

"Jehudiel, no," I began.

The archangel raised his hand, silencing me. "We all have our burdens to bear."

"But your people have been here for over a year."

He nodded.

"They're going to drain you dry. And after you're gone they will still die," I said.

He nodded again. "We must only hold on for a little longer. After this mission, I have a feeling things will change forever. My life is worthless without purpose. My people are my burden to bear. I was the one who broke off and rallied them. It falls to me to sustain them."

"Surely there must be another way," I said. "Wait, what about Anael? She's an archangel too, maybe together you can-"

"No!"

Thunder rolled with his voice. Jehudiel looked up and sighed.

"I am sorry," he said calmly. "But no. Anael must be at full strength. She will lead once I have expired. This is not her sacrifice to make but mine."

Angels, man, I tell you.

"However," he went on. "Once this way-station is destroyed, Gabriel's forces will have no means of invading. Our mission here will end soon. Now come, we must join the others."

We walked back together. All the while I couldn't bat away a thought: will the mission end before it claimed Jehudiel's life?

"Is this really necessary?" Greede complained, as Emrys refastened a bracelet around his right hand. "You are sending me into enemy territory unarmed and crippled. You might as well kill me now."

"Don't tempt me," Emrys said.

We were inside a tent, with a map of a large field containing a single silo-like building.

"The way-station," said Jehudiel. "They usually are a means of transporting energy in between points, but this one has been modified to allow personnel to travel to and fro. And this is how you will infiltrate Heaven and retrieve the Sword of Michael."

He pointed at the surrounding area. Little blobs of blue light rose up.

"However, it is the most heavily guarded angelic ground in the world. We have been trying to skirmish it for months to no avail. Our efforts have only led to more fortifications."

Amaymon chuckled. "Good thing you got yourselves a battering ram then."

He popped his knuckles.

Jehudiel nodded at him. "There will be carnage. This is unavoidable. However, those troops are still my brothers."

"I got me a couple brothers too," Amaymon said. "Don't worry, I'll be real nice. Right until I get through them."

Jehudiel sighed. "It is inevitable," he murmured. Then in his regular voice,

"Very well. Amaymon will lead the assault through the front." He indicated on the map. "My team and I shall flank here and here. The Grigori will aid us."

Emrys nodded. "All except me. I have another duty to perform," he said. "To retrieve the Spear of the Sun."

Jehudiel nodded. "Very well. The Slime and the Golem can be here. The Kresnik and Pyromancer, here. Anael will bring the rear."

Amaymon snickered.

"Oh come on, it was right there!"

"You are a child," I told him. Then to Jehudiel, "Okay, so me and... ah, shit."

"Hi," Greede said.

"I don't want to babysit him," I said.

"You won't have to," Greede said. "Because there is a tiny little flaw with the plan."

We all glared at him.

"Do tell," Emrys said icily.

"As soon as Erik and myself enter Heaven, the angels present *there* will sense the intrusion and kill us," he said. "We need a disguise. Something good enough to fool angelic senses."

He grinned.

"Lucky for you I have just the item. Mr. Emrys, would it be possible for you to access the inventory of items you have pilfered from me?"

The Druid shook his head. "I don't have access to that. Not that there's much left."

Greede sighed. "Of course. You barbarians failed to grasp the scope of my projects and thus had them destroyed. Millenia of knowledge, gone up in smoke. In that case, I will need you to remove this cuff."

"Not a chance," Emrys said.

"It is the only way I can access the Necronomicon, in which I have kept a backup of all my successful projects for just such an occasion," Greede said. "Unless of course, you have a better idea, in which case I am listening. Oh, and tick-tock, Mr. Druid. Belphegor waits for no one."

Emrys looked like he was about to be sick. Then, he gave Greg a nod, and the Kresnik reluctantly seized Greede's wrist to undo the lock on the cuff bracelet.

"Thank you," Greede said, massaging his wrist.

"I warn you, Greede," Emrys began.

"Yes, yes, big hole, never see the light of day... You made yourself perfectly clear the first time, I assure you." He clasped his hands together and I felt magic swirl around him.

An instant later he was holding the Necronomicon, a thick black leather-bound tome that was also one of the most dangerous magical artifacts in history.

Greede flipped through it as if he was leafing through a magazine and finally said,

"Ah, yes. Project SA-23B."

He unceremoniously tore the page and made the rest of the book disappear. Then he waved the page in the air.

"I only have enough for two so we'll have to make it count," he said. When he stopped waving the page, two vials were in his hand in its place.

A brilliant blue color pulsed from within the vials.

"SA stands for Synthetic Angel," he explained. "After I extracted Ezekiel's Grace, I managed to replicate it. It only works on base-line humans, so I'm afraid most of you are out, except for myself, Mr. Ashendale, and Mr. Emrys. The latter will be going, so that leaves the choices obvious."

He picked one, pressed a button, ejecting a needle, and stabbed the vial in his thigh. As the liquid coursed through his veins, a blue light went through his entire being, ending with an explosion of ethereal light behind him that took the shape of angelic wings. They disappeared a flash later, leaving only a blue-white glow in his eyes.

"Since I'm just a regular Joe it will last an hour in me," he said. "In you, Erik, given your enhanced power, I would wager half that time. Provided you do not overtly use any magic, we should be able to sneak in and out unnoticed in half an hour."

He handed me the vial, needle already protruding.

I looked at it, then at Greede.

If only he'd used his brilliant mind for good, the world would have been a thousand times better.

But instead, he was selfish and dangerous. The Grace he had extracted by literally pulling out the still-beating heart of an archangel, the Virtue that countered his original Sin, Greed.

I stabbed the vial in my leg and felt a rush of power go through me. But instead of elation, all I got was weight. The power felt heavy, like I had to hold it steady against a current that was unrelenting.

Greede had given me half an hour. It would be a feat if I held onto it for that long.

Grimacing, I looked at the rest of them.

"Come on. Let's get going."

10

Say what you will about us: we know how to make an entrance.

Amaymon was the first to pop out. The angels—about fifty of them, wielding glowing lances, bows and arrows, crossbows, glaives and swords—flared their wings and turned their attention towards the demon.

He did not disappoint.

"S'up, mothafuckas!"

Screaming like a berserker, he leapt out of the ground, grabbed two angels by the head and slammed them down.

Behind him, the rogue angels erupted from tunnels that Amaymon had created. They surged at the enemy, taking them by surprise.

From the rear of the silo, screams erupted as more angels led by Anael divided the silo's guard. I spotted Luke's fiery form zooming in the air, spraying fireballs all over the enemy while presumably Evans was doing his best Hulk Smash impression.

From our side, Seneschal and Greg ambushed a side door. Greg's spear fighting was accurate and surgical. I had never seen Seneschal fight, and thank god for that. The Slime surged from his clothing, and wrapped himself around his opponent's waist, leaving a trail of spores in his wake. The spores took over the angel, pushing him to his knees, while Seneschal reformed, grabbed the angel's head and pulled it off with relative ease.

The inside had already been hollowed out by the spores.

I tried not to throw up. It tends to disrupt delicate magic like the illusion spell I was holding over Greede and myself.

Greg smashed the door open, revealing the silo to be empty.

"The diversion worked," Greede murmured. In order for both of us to be covered we had to stand very close. The man was practically breathing in my ear.

Opting to remain silent rather than knock his teeth out, I pulled us inwards. The room was white and sterile as was all angelic architecture, with a single pair of sliding doors ahead of us. Through the glass, I saw a ramp of bright white light.

I dissolved the illusion and fished out the key card Anael had given me. As soon as it touched my skin, the plastic of the card turned bright white. I felt it pull at the angelic powers inside of me, and gritted my teeth against the discomfort.

We had to get this over with.

I slid the card into the slot and it beeped. The sliding doors parted.

"Go," Greg said. "We'll guard the entrance."

I nodded at him and grabbed Greede's upper arm.

"Stay close. You try anything and I'll make it hurt," I told him.

"Please don't kill me in Heaven," he said. "The last thing I want is an afterlife with those boring things."

The portal was not a usual portal but a stream of energy. It tilted upwards almost like a ramp. White light streamed upwards like lightning being channeled in neat, narrow beams. As soon as I stepped in it, I felt it connect to the Synthetic Angel serum in my veins, likely registering me as a friendly.

Which was why, instead of being vaporized on the spot, I was yanked upwards.

My physical form melded away into bright white light, and the last thing I saw was Greede undergoing a similar experience—except he grinned and gave me a thumbs-up.

I flipped him off as we were yanked into Heaven.

Last time I had been in Heaven it had been to witness Raphael's execution. At that time, the plane had been bright and high, and impossibly massive. It had been beyond the scope of words simply because human words could not encompass the majesty that lay before me. I had also had to be enshrouded in Jehudiel's aura (along with wearing some dope sunglasses) in order to protect me from the sheer power of the place.

Greede's synthetic power eliminated the need for that, but I don't even think we needed it.

Heaven was... *less.*

That is the only way I could think to describe it. It was less of everything—less white, less bright, less beautiful, less orderly, less powerful.

It was like watching the end of an empire, the withering of a once-great forest, as it was reduced to a mere fraction of what it once was.

The platform we arrived on was solid marble. All around us were angels in formation, no doubt awaiting orders. The walls were thick and reinforced, and I immediately likened where we were to a barracks of sorts.

Gabriel had turned his home plane into one giant fortification. Such was the scope of Heaven's magic—one angel with sufficient power could terraform the whole place.

Greede pulled me aside and out of sight.

"Stay focused, Erik," he hissed. "It wouldn't do to get caught now."

He plucked out another page from the Necronomicon—he had kept the book on his person since I wouldn't unlock his power-dampening bracelet—and pressed the spell into my chest.

My black coat changed color, turning white. His suit did the same thing, along with his hair, and his eyes—blue under the synthetic angel formula—glowed blue and remained like that.

"Now you fit in," he said.

I nodded and tried to get my head in the game. I had been underestimating how dire our situation was. I had been seeing the enemy in trickles, groups that were sent to hunt me down. But this...

This was an entire world's populace uniformly determined towards a singular goal. And I had just walked into their stronghold.

I shook my head. *Focus, Erik. Focus on the Sword. In and out, no problems.*

I looked up and closed my eyes. Reaching out with my magic, I could tell where the most spikes in power came from. Thankfully the synthetic angel formula made it so that not every single angel felt like a supernova. I could rifle through power signatures with ease.

But using my magic cost me. I could feel the formula

wearing off, and my energy signature starting to break through.

"Damn!" Greede swore. He ran off while I was still struggling and I heard him say,

"Over here!"

He returned with two angel soldiers. I glared at him and reached for Djinn. At least I could take him down with me.

As the angels approached, Greede stayed behind them. His fingers were tensed into claws, holding a shredded piece of paper between them. A pair of purple-black nooses of energy wrapped themselves around the angels' necks. He tightened but they were struggling.

"Now!" he strained.

I slammed the pommel of my sword into one angel's head, knocking him out, while swiping at the other's sword and elbowing him in the face.

Both went down.

Greede released his magic. "Good god, man," he said, panting. "Could you be any slower?"

"I didn't know your serum was so delicate," I retorted.

"There's nothing wrong with my serum," he snapped. "It's you. Your magic is out of alignment with anything I have ever encountered." He sighed. "It's a good thing I came along. You won't be able to handle something like the Sword of Michael. It's too holy for you."

I was about to say something, when I remembered a little incident that had occurred last year.

During a fight, Greg had dropped his spear, which was imbued with a metric ton of holy magic. I went to pick it up and got severely burned by it. This had concerned Greg since I was supposed to be human but something inside me clearly wasn't.

"We'll see when we get to it," I told him. "Let's get there first."

"Right." He nodded. Then he looked at the unconscious angels. "And them?"

I cocked my head. "What about them?"

"They will wake up and raise the alarm," Greede said. "We should kill them."

"No," I told Greede.

The latter sighed.

I never saw the pair of ethereal daggers manifest. Only after they shot out, one into each of the angels' necks, severing their throats and spilling golden ichor on the white floor did I become aware of them.

I rushed Greede and grabbed him by the collar.

"What did you do?" I slammed him into a wall and pressed Djinn's blade to his throat, see how he liked it.

He remained calm, his blue eyes frigid. "I did what you are too sentimental to do, Erik. I made sure our mission succeeds. They are the enemy."

"I said no killing."

"A wrong choice."

"I swear, Greede-"

"Spare me," he said. "Your threats are meaningless. If you attack me, your presence will be revealed and our mission will fail. You need me and I need you. So what say you we get that Sword and get out of here as quickly as possible. I promise you can resume your petty feud with me once we are clear."

Goddammit he was right.

I lowered the sword and let him go.

"Excellent," he said, adjusting his suit. "Now then, let's hope your magic was worth it. Lead away, Mr. Ashendale."

11

Michael's quarters were at the summit of a tall spiral-like building just outside the barracks.

Entering was easy enough. To most angels we looked like slightly rugged troops. Unlike the last time I had been here, not all angels wore armor. In their home some wore tunics, some had coats like mine and others had variations of modern-day clothing.

It wasn't supposed to be like this. Heaven had changed. Order—the thing that defined this place—was no longer as tight as it had once been. And unlike Earth, where things lived in a balance, even a slight tilt in the world order here would be...

Well, apocalyptic.

Greede and I made it towards the top, and that was when things got itchy.

Suddenly we were surrounded by eight angels in full armor and wings spread wide. A royal guard of some kind. The top of the top, guarding their leader's place of rest.

"Halt!" said one of them. His lance was pointing uncomfortably close to my face. "Why are you here?"

I glanced at Greede. He was the sweet talker of the group.

"We were sent here," he told the guard. "Official business from Gabriel himself."

"State your business," the guard said.

"None of yours," Greede said. I shot him a glare. He shrugged.

The tension doubled. "You are acting strangely," another of the guards said. "I sense something in you..." Now he looked at me.

And right then, my synthetic angel power just *stopped*.

I was already holding onto it with slippery fingers, and now...

POOF.

Regular human in an angelic stronghold—a *wanted* human at that.

Their eyes widened.

I swept Djinn across the closest guard's lance, slashing him at the shoulder. I felt another lance stab me in the back, just as the wielder screamed when Greede blasted him with purple energy. The spell did very little damage to the angel, who backhanded Greede and sent him flying.

I pulled out my gun with my left hand and started firing shots.

An alarm went off, blaring out like a raiding siren.

More swords and spears slashed and cut into me. Somehow my weapons went flying, and the lead guard hefted a broadsword in my direction.

I called on my power, and black shadows exploded from around me. A pair of shadowy arms clamped around the blade and held it in place, while I lunged upwards and delivered an uppercut to the angel. At the same time, four more tendrils shot out. Three were either cut or evaded but a fourth landed and slammed said angel into the wall with enough force to go through. The angel was sent tumbling down the spiral.

As more shadows emerged from me, I heard Greede tear another page and mutter a spell. My heightened senses picked up on the subtleties of his magic; how he was enhancing the shadows and spreading them, bathing the corridor in darkness.

The only light was coming from the angels and Djinn, whose blade glowed azure when I retrieved it. Holding onto the ring that served as a guard, I poured magic into the weapon and created a clone of it in my left hand, both weapons attached by the pommel with a length of ethereal cord.

I charged at the angels like a whirlwind, slicing and stabbing. At one point the clone sword met a particularly vicious spear and shattered, forcing me to flip the angel in question and pummel him into the ground with my fists and elbows.

I felt something hard against my knee and realized it was my gun. Retrieving the weapon, I charged magic into it and when I fired, the bullet split in two, hitting two angels at the same time. It clipped them, nothing lethal, but it was enough for me to get close and finish the job.

Eight angels down, one injured Erik, and a stunned Greede massaging a welt growing at the back of his head.

His shadow spell dissipated, and I punched the door in, knocking it off the hinges.

Michael's quarters were...

Very small.

There was a four-poster bed, a table, a chair, a fireplace that was devoid of any flame, and a bookshelf with a small stack of books.

As I walked in I willed my shadows back. My coat had

also turned black again, signifying that I was truly back to human with no other active spell on or in me at all.

In other words, I was on my own.

Greede looked around. "It's too small."

"The guy is an angel," I said. "Maybe it's a lifestyle choice."

He shook his head. "No. The magic. There is too much here for what we are seeing." Then he smiled. "Ah, but of course."

With a wave of his hands, he summoned the Necronomicon again and found the spell he was looking for. Tearing the page, he flourished it and released it into the air where it exploded into a million cinders.

Everywhere those cinders landed, reality rippled and burned away, starting with tiny holes and growing, until the whole room peeled away, and we were standing in front of a massive pool of water. In the middle of the pool, like a fountain statue, was a mannequin adorned with the most beautiful set of armor I had ever seen. It looked like solid water: light and heavy at the same time. The color changed, picked ambient light and reflected it as if through a kaleidoscope.

I looked down.

Submerged in the water was a flaming sword. It rested on a bench of white marble—a broadsword of pure orange fire, still burning even though it was submerged.

Without thinking, I went to step into the water.

Only I couldn't.

I could see my foot landing in the pool, but before I could make contact with the water, I was back on solid ground.

"Another illusion?" I asked.

I could see Greede shaking his head in my peripheral

vision. "Too much power for any spell to take. This is the real thing."

I called on my powers. Shadows swirled around me. I stepped into the pool.

Light flared and there was a ringing, savage screaming in my ears. I realized it was me, roaring in agony and an influx of emotion as every neuron in my head fired. I couldn't move forward nor go backward—there was just pain and agony, and no promise of it ending any time soon.

It was Greede who stopped it.

Greede who stepped into the pool, calm and casual, unaffected by the water, and reached the Sword.

Water rose higher suddenly, submerging the both of us. The pain left as quickly as it had come but I was still rooted to the spot.

In front of us was the Sword. Except it was the size of a building. Easily three stories high, its fiery glare was dulled by the water.

Greede was inches from the handle. He reached out.

The Sword shuddered and flared, and the water evaporated as immense heat and fire consumed the world. This wasn't just intense flame either. This was primordial.

This was the Big Bang and the end of the universe all wrapped in one giant sword.

There was a speck of black. A speck in the shape of a book.

An instant later we were back in that pool, Greede half-submerged in water, with the Necronomicon in his hands. The page it was open on had a drawing of the Sword of Michael, the edges of the ink glowing with heat and magic.

He closed the book.

"How did you do that?" I asked.

"The Necronomicon is a prison," he explained, walking

out of the water. "I simply imprisoned the Sword within." He shrugged. "Guess my theory was right. Now all we have to do is get it back home."

He started walking away. I rushed after him, and made sure to stay close.

The last thing I wanted was to lose a psychopath with a magical nuclear weapon.

12

Our journey down the spiral was *not* uneventful. In fact it was very eventful.

Angels-with-bazookas eventful.

They blew up the floor beneath us. Greede and I became separated with rubble between us. One of my legs was crushed under a boulder. My healing magic took over instantly. I suppose there's an upside to having a family curse: instant healing.

Doesn't stop it from hurting like a son of a bitch.

The world spun in front of me, and I remembered that the angels I was seeing weren't the fluffy kind but the weapon-wielding murderous kind. Just my luck—I mean who goes to Heaven and ends up being hunted by angels?

A tendril of shadows swatted away an oncoming angel, while I hobbled on my injured leg, Djinn in hand and gun in the other. I wrapped my legs in shadows and magically enhanced my leap.

Black wings emerged from my back, spreading out.

I couldn't help but grin. Over the past year I had spent every free moment practicing with my shadows. I was aware it was Life Magic, but other than that, there was virtually no information. I mean, if my sister—the family bookworm—couldn't figure it out, what chance did a blockhead like me have?

But I could practice and get familiar with it, hence why I was flying around through Heaven, chased by flabbergasted angels. I hugged one side of the spiral, and zoomed up.

I turned abruptly and released two spells at once, one from each of my channels. The gun roared, the trio of bullets released replicating and raining down on my pursuers.

The angels zoomed past them, easily evading the bright-red bullets.

They never saw the tiny black bullet made entirely out of shadows.

In the meantime, I released a slash of energy from Djinn, sending the spell streaking along a wide area. The angels scattered, forming a line to avoid the streak.

I grinned.

"Now you see me-"

I teleported.

Spatial magic had never been my specialty. When I had not had my magic (technically I had but I hadn't been able to cast any spells, only having access to my healing magic—thank you, family curse) teleportation has been something of a fantasy. Even now, with access to my magic again, I still couldn't do the regular version.

But I could do spatial swaps, especially if a portion of my shadows had been fired past the angels and now hovered behind them.

I popped out behind them, replacing that small black bullet, and charged Djinn up again.

"Now you don't!"

The second streak, even larger than the first, sandwiched the angels and pulverized them.

So much for non-lethal action.

The blast of magic blew past the angels and crashed into the side of the spiral. A building-sized groove was lashed open, and the spiral tilted slightly.

"Ashendale!"

Greede's scream came from inside the spiral—he was still trapped in there—and I rushed through the hole I had just created and barreled into an unfortunate angel that was just finding his feet. He went swaying and dropped back on the ground.

"Sorry," I called back, zooming towards Greede's voice.

I also didn't bother with walls, which was how I knocked over a sword-wielding angel viciously striking at Greede.

The latter spun, twin flaming swords in hand—which I later recognized as miniature versions of the Sword of Michael—and stabbed both of them into the chest of a second angel.

"Took you long enough," he said.

I had never seen Greede this disheveled or exhausted. He slumped against a wall. The swords evaporated from his hands.

"You figured out how the Sword works?" I asked.

He shook his head. "I merely copied ten percent of its properties and conjured a pair of clones."

"In other words, cheap imitations."

"It did the job, didn't it?"

That it did. Greede had never been a frontline fighter but judging by the number of dead angels, I had to be impressed.

Yet another ace up his sleeve.

The spiral shook again.

"It's the same artillery that blew up the top half," he explained. "They are perched on two adjacent buildings." He exhaled in exhaustion. "I don't have enough magic to both teleport there and kill them. Never mind two places."

Boom!

The spiral rocked again.

A plan formed in my mind.

"How effective are those swords of yours?" I asked. "And how many can you conjure?"

"You can't play with my toys, Ashendale," he said with a weak smile.

"Then you play with them."

Without waiting for him to get up, I snatched him and held him under one arm. Then I focused my shadowy wings to beat and fly, and we went out zooming outside the spiral.

"Now, Greede. Sword time!"

Suspended in my hands, Greede conjured his swords again and lanced through the first angel in our way. He threw them, conjured two more and sent them firing at another oncoming angel.

From the distance I could see the pair of angels on a building fussing over an ornate cannon of sorts. It looked like something out of the Civil War, but with more gold and way too much decorative filigree.

I made a beeline straight for the cannon and when I was close enough, I covered Greede with shadows and literally tossed him head—or sword, in this case—first towards the angels. Hopefully my magic was going to keep him in one piece.

If not...

Ah, well, too bad. Accidents happen.

I landed on the second angel, punching him so hard he was sent flying, and brought my sword down on the cannon, cleaving it in half.

Then before more angels could converge on us, Greede tossed a little ball of purple light on the fuse, and we ran.

The cannon exploded just as the angels reached us, blasting them all to smithereens.

"We're out of range of the second one," I told Greede. "There's the way-station." I closed my eyes and pictured my familiar. "Amaymon, can you hear me?"

The demon's voice was distant. He had warned me that the closer we got to the way-station the better reception I would get. We were only two blocks away but he sounded so hazy and distant.

"I'm here... where... know..."

"We need to get closer," I told Greede.

He looked like he was about to have a heart attack, and never took his eyes off the streets below. When I looked down I understood why.

It was a sea of angels, all of them looking at us, all of them holding weapons.

All of them ready to kill us.

I closed my eyes again and focused on the connection. "Be ready. We're coming through. Keep the way open."

Luckily this time the message went through. "Loud and clear, boss."

I opened my eyes again. "The way is open," I told Greede. Then grimacing, "Now we just have to get there."

Greede turned green. "That is a lot of enemies."

"It is."

He sighed. "Just in case we die today, Mr. Ashendale, I want you to know..."

I raised an eyebrow at him.

"I have always hated you."

I chuckled. "Likewise. Now put your game face on. Time to get ourselves back home."

13

When faced with overwhelming odds, you only get two choices. You can either run away or charge headfirst. I was never one to run away. To be fair, I'm nigh-immortal and have more magic than any Wizard I've ever encountered. Heck, I was beating angels on their home turf.

But Greede was a runner.

Fortunately, he ran in the right direction.

Screaming his head off, he had the Necronomicon open, and was tearing out pages left and right, mutilating the book as he made his escape. A plethora of spells hit the angels.

Some turned into animals before reverting back seconds later feeling very confused, others found the ground before them melted; one time a meteor the size of a football fell down and took out several dozen. Bolts of magic in all shapes and colors shot from all over him.

All that to get over just one block.

Suddenly he stopped and slumped down. An angel struck him with a sword in the leg and then another thwacked him in the head with the blunt end of his spear.

Another would have killed him had I not disarmed him. Literally.

"My turn," I told Greede as I landed besides him and used shadows to wrap him up and levitate him.

Shadows flared from my body, forming bulky armor and turning my shortsword in to a massive double-hander. Behind me, a second Knightmare formed, a spectral construct that protected Greede and watched my back.

A spiked tower shield formed in my left hand and I charged. Time and space warped around me as I literally dug into the fabric of reality to hoist myself forward. My shield took massive damage but it held. The spectral knight lost its head—luckily it didn't need it.

Greede was helping out by firing dagger-sized Swords of Michael, seriously crippling anyone the knight missed.

A vicious series of blows by no less than five angels broke my broadsword. I turned the shattered blade into shards that tore into them and reformed the sword. The effect was taxing and just as I reached the entrance to the way-station, I felt my magic falter.

My injured leg was giving out—I simply did not have enough magic to sustain both the healing and the plethora of magic I was using. My healing had slowed down since I started using regular magic—there was always a price to pay.

I forced Greede in before me, and dissolved my armor, pouring everything into the spectral knight and ordering it to bar the door. It did its best, but a cannon blast tore through it and sent me and Greede flying away from the white stream of light that was our way home.

I had been wrong. The cannon could reach us.

Stupid, Erik. In my haste I had cut corners. Now I was going to pay for it.

Greede made it to the stream but hissed as it burned him.

"We ran out of synth-angel formula," he said. "We can't go back. We can't- OUFFF!"

A massive fist of stone and rock wrapped itself around Greede and dragged him into the light. I heard his muffled screams as he disappeared.

Amaymon partially emerged from the stream of white light that served as a portal.

He looked severely injured. His hair was burnt and half his face was just raw nerves. Some of his jaw bone was exposed.

Worse, his human guise had been torn apart, forcing him to assume a hybrid of his original appearance. Cat hair covered the parts that were not burnt, along with a single cat ear (the other was ash). A pair of rock arms that usually came out of his back when in demonic form, were now burnt to stumps. He was struggling to reform them and reach me.

"Amaymon, it's killing you," I said. "Go back."

The demon grimaced. "Not without you, Erik."

The angels were stunned. I could see the uncertainty in their eyes. Finally, someone yelled, "Kill it!" and they charged.

I was faster.

I put everything I had into a blast from Djinn. The beam of azure energy cut through the angels, nowhere near enough to hurt them but enough to make them pause.

I threw myself face forwards at Amaymon who grabbed me and forcibly pulled me down and down...

And down.

. . .

BOOM!

The stream of white light stopped dragging me down and instead we were thrown sideways. It was like riding a train and suddenly you were off the tracks. There was no up or down, left or right.

We hurtled through space and time, with Amaymon hugging me as close to him as possible, until reality spat us back out.

I TUMBLED on burnt grass in the middle of a war zone. I recognized the outside of the way-station on Earth, and angels flying, battling each other. The rogue faction was losing. Many of their numbers were bleeding ichor around me. From the distance I heard Greg yell something. Greede was struggling against Seneschal who had attached itself to both his hands to prevent him from casting.

I stood up and tried not to heave.

"Amaymon," I croaked. My throat was so dry. I could not feel my familiar's presence. "Amaymon!"

I saw him next to me.

Amaymon was in his demonic form. The last time I had seen him like this was when he had battled the Demon Emperor. He had been the size of a modest skyscraper.

Now, he was no larger than a Maine Coon. His stony back arms were brittle and flaked at my touch. His paws were burnt, the long-clawed fingers sheared off. Half his hair was singed away. His twin tails had been cut off, while the series of crystals along his spine were now mere protrusions.

"Amaymon!" I went to him and could not hear him breathe. Not that demons breathed.

I shook him. "Amaymon?" Something round and heavy and thick was in my throat. My hands started shaking.

"Amaymon, wake up!"

Ignoring the battle overhead, I closed my eyes and reached for my magic. Anything would do, even the last dregs that were keeping me alive. Anything to help him.

But I had nothing. I was an empty tank. Ignoring my own injuries, I struggled to get up and call for help.

Crack.

It was a small sound but I heard it like a gong going off in my head.

The ruby pendant that Amaymon always wore—he had even affixed it on his collar as a cat—had a massive crack in it from top to bottom. I touched the pendant.

This was our pact made physical. That pendant, which I wore but had given to him as a symbol of freedom, was what bound us together, what allowed him to live on Earth without needing to return to Hell.

It was his life force.

And it was broken.

Amaymon was dying and I couldn't help him.

"Help," I cried, my voice barely audible in the din. "Someone help. Someone. *Help! Help us!* AMAYMON!"

There was a soft flash of light and she emerged. A tall elfin woman wearing yellow and green and carrying a spear. Her mane of wheat-colored hair was braided, which made her emerald eyes sparkle. As she kneeled down next to Amaymon I noted her tapered ears.

A Fey.

She smiled at me and pressed her hands on him. I felt magic flow from her as she reached into the earth itself and renewed the connection between Amaymon's elemental nature and the earth he drew strength from.

Amaymon's eyes, bloodshot and broken, fluttered.

"Amaymon," I said.

Before I could reach him, another Fey, this one tall and dark, wielding a pair of longswords, came over to us.

"We must move, Niamh," she said. "The Druid comes." She rolled her eyes. "Bear Down Protocol."

"Understood," Niamh said. With inconceivable strength she raised Amaymon in a cradle hold and walked away.

I followed them.

"What's going on? Where are you taking him?" I asked. "Hey, where are you taking my familiar?"

"Quiet, human," the dark Fey said. "We must move or we will get caught in the crossfire. Niamh will keep healing your demon. I shall protect you."

Niamh offered me a weak smile, as she set Amaymon down on the ground. "You will forgive Morgana's bedside manner." And she went back to healing.

Morgana chuckled. "Here he comes. He does like this bit."

CAW!

An eagle soared over the battling angels, most of whom were only being kept at bay thanks to the Grigori. There was just over a dozen angels now, no more coming thanks to Amaymon's destruction of the way-station, but they were starting to overwhelm our forces.

CAW!

The eagle circled lower and lower.

CAW!

It went into a nose dive.

ROAR!

The eagle was replaced by a brown bear the size of a Sherman tank, which landed flatly on top of three angels there were now in definite need of a chiropractor.

The bear swatted away several other angels, each blow of its paws enhanced with the same magic Niamh was using to heal Amaymon.

The bear rolled into an enemy, leapt, and morphed.

Emrys, wearing green leathers, somersaulted and, when he landed, slammed the butt of a spear down on the ground.

It was a magnificent weapon, a fiery gold with a wide wavy blade. Like the Sword of Michael, it looked like it was made out of liquid fire, but where that one was regal, this one was wild and untamed.

Upon slamming the pommel to the ground, a flare of fire and magic blasted the angels into ashes, also throwing back the Grigori. Even Luke, who was a Pyromancer and literally on fire, had to bat away the golden flames.

When he stood up, Emrys turned the spear into something small enough to fit into his pocket and rushed towards us.

"The demon is critical," Niamh said. "I am reaching the limits of my healing ability."

"He requires a proper facility," Morgana said.

"The mansion," I said. "We have to take him there."

Niamh nodded and stepped away, allowing me to pick him up. I felt Amaymon shudder in my arms. He was weak, I could tell. Unless I hurried, I was going to lose another family member.

"Erik," he said weakly.

"Hey," I said. "Don't worry, we're getting you all fixed up. That was one badass explosion, wasn't it?"

He chuckled. "I kicked them angels' asses." His stone arms struggled for a moment and before I could stop him, he was pressing the ruby pendant into my chest. He managed to loop it around my neck with a painful sigh.

"You take care of that for a while."

"Amaymon?"

He did not reply. Holding him tight, I rushed towards a portal Emrys had opened before it was too late.

14

The coffee cup shook in my hands. The shot of whiskey someone had put in it (Greg perhaps, I genuinely had no recollection) was not working.

All I could do was sit there in front of a tank filled with eerie greenish liquid, while Amaymon's form hung floating in the midst of it. Crystals and mud caked the bottom, some of the crystals growing visibly as Amaymon's demonic blood mixed in with the vat's liquid. The doctors and xeno-biologists in the mansion's staff said that was a positive sign but I didn't put too much faith in their words. These were the same people who had diagnosed my curse and had no clue what they had been talking about back then.

Like me, Amaymon was unique, and his condition was severe.

The coffee cup would not stop shaking in my hands.

I heard the door open and then close behind me. Footsteps approached. Abi sat next to me.

"He's going to make it."

I remained silent.

"I mean, this is Amaymon we are talking about. Never

mind the fact he's a primordial demon—you can never get rid of the guy," she went on. It would have been a convincing performance if only her voice didn't break halfway through the sentence.

I was still holding the pendant, and opened my fist to show her the broken ruby.

"He came for me," I told her. "He must have known that bridge would be deadly to him. But he still came. And he fought the angels. He pulled me out, rigged the explosion, and now look…"

I held the ruby in front of her.

"It's cracked," she said. "Damaged but not broken."

I stood up and the coffee cup went flying. It smashed against a wall somewhere in the gloom of the room, bathing the space with the ringing sound of anger.

I stood up and pressed my free hand on Amaymon's tank. It was cool to the touch.

Cold.

Dead.

"Erik?" Abi was next to me. Her soft hands pressed on my shoulders. She hesitated when she felt me shaking. "Erik, he's not dead. He's still here. Look. He's not gone."

"She is right," came Anael's voice from behind.

I turned to look at her. The angel had assumed her human form again. She walked all the way up to the tank and pressed a finger along the edge of it.

"The demon is still bound to you, Erik," she said. "He is weak. He needs rest. But Amaymon is not yet lost. No mere angel can do that, not even the concentrated holy energy that makes the bridge. It would weaken him but not kill him."

"They're gonna pay for this," I said. "Gabriel and his

whole fucking team. They are gonna be sorry they ever came after me."

Anael's eyes were hypnotizing. "You are in agony over your loss, and you respond with the easiest emotion to you: anger."

"This is the second family member your species has taken away from me," I snapped.

"Killing Gabriel will only make Sloth stronger," she said. "And it will create a void to be filled by another like Gabriel. Perhaps someone more dogmatic and ruthless than he has become."

"Then what do you propose?" I turned fully towards her, towering over her.

"Tell me, Angel of Love, what shall I do? Forgive? Make peace? It may have escaped your attention during our sessions, but every time I find love, destruction follows. So maybe I'm not meant for love. Maybe I'm meant to find your kin and break them, until Amaymon feels better and Gil is returned."

I felt Abi grab me from behind. I turned. Her open palm struck me so hard I stumbled.

With tears in her eyes, she marched out of the room.

"She too has turbulent feelings," Anael said.

"Shut up," I told her, nursing my bruise. It was already healing but the shock still remained.

"Have you ever stopped to consider her emotions?" Anael went on. "A succubus falling in love—that is bound to raise some questions, is it not? Especially one with a conscience as big as Abi's."

"What the fuck are you talking about?"

"Oh, do pull your head out of your ass," Anael snapped. "Why do you think I hang around Abi so much? Like I told you the day I helped you unlock your powers: I go where I am needed. Abi has been struggling with her love for you. She needed counsel. Now, I suspect she feels betrayed."

I sat back down. My heart hurt, it was pounding so hard against my chest. Somehow I felt even worse than I had five minutes ago.

"You will go talk to her," Anael said. "You will not shut yourself off."

"Anael," I told her. "Go away."

The angel gave me one hard look, then with the fluttering of wings she departed.

When I emerged from the room, it was dark. I followed the sound of arguing and found the Grigori in a meeting room. Abi was there. She saw me enter and averted her gaze.

That annoyed me more. Look, if she had doubts about being with me, then she should have said something earlier. We've been together for a year. I thought we were fine.

Guess she didn't think so.

Either way, I didn't have time for this.

"What's going on?" I asked.

Emrys looked up. "How is he?"

"About as good as someone lifelessly suspended in a tank can be," I said, keeping my voice cold. "What is going on here?"

I looked around me.

All the Grigori were gathered. Most of them were in various states of healing. Jack fussed over a bandage on Luke's arm who rolled his eyes but let him carry on. Greg had his forearm in a splint. He was sipping from a potion that smelled like boiled cabbage and fermented garlic. Seneschal sat in a basin, his lower body pure jelly. The Slime even looked smaller. Evans was nowhere to be seen.

Likely the real Evans (a wheelchair-bound foul-mouthed Jew with a genius IQ and a penchant for building golems) had directed the big battle golem away for some private repair.

Mustafa, who had clearly just arrived, straightened his mustache when I walked in. I resisted the urge to knock off his turban. We disliked each other but kept it civil. His two aides, dark-skinned beauties wrapped in traditional silk dresses, carried his luggage.

Speaking of pretty females, Niamh and Morgana also sat on a couch. They were a study in contrasts: Niamh sat regally poised, while Morgana slouched backwards, a bottle of liquor in her hand.

Anael stood in her battle suit, minus the wings and radiance, beside Turtle who was happily munching away from a tray of biscuits.

Greede sat behind a table on a leather office chair that would have presumably been occupied by my sister.

"We were having a discussion," Emrys said. "On how best to store the Keys."

"A discussion?" I asked. "Why is it even a discussion?"

Greede leaned forward. "Because not everyone can-"

BLAM!

I lowered my gun from where I had fired into the upper right corner of the ceiling and aimed it towards Greede.

The entire room went dead silent. I felt everyone tense up.

"Like I said," I said, "this is not a discussion. You keep that Sword, you get a bullet. Three..."

"The energy required would kill the wielder," he protested.

"Erik, let's talk about this," Emrys said.

"TWO!" I pulled Greede up by his sweater and pressed

the barrel of the gun against his right eyeball.

"Erik, if you kill him, we lose the Sword," Greg shouted.

"This is not the way, Erik," Anael added.

"Erik, we need to find a way to contain it safely before-" Emrys began.

"ONE!"

The thumbing of my hammer echoed like thunderclap. Suddenly, I was aware of several weapons being pointed at me, from Anael's two-pronged spear, to Niamh's leaf-shaped one, Morgana's swords, Turtle's staff, and Luke's finger which was heated up and ready to fire a laser at me.

Greede was shaking.

"Give. Us. The. Sword." I said.

"I can't," he whispered.

"Not a good answer."

"I'm not lying," he said. "I can extract it from the Necronomicon but it will revert to its original size. Do you remember how big it was?"

I said nothing.

"It will also act as a beacon, calling to all the forces of Heaven until it is returned to its rightful place," he went on. "Emrys will tell you. So will the angel. I am not lying."

I tilted my head backwards and looked at Anael while ignoring her spear.

"He speaks the truth," she said. "Lower your weapon."

"Erik," Emrys said. "Please. I know you're hurting. But we have to see this through. Otherwise, Amaymon's sacrifice was for nothing. Please. Let him go."

I lowered my gun and tossed Greede back into the chair. He rolled backwards until Morgana kicked him away from her.

Then I walked out, my stomach tight and the pressure in my chest feeling like it was about to explode.

15

I kept walking, headed for nowhere. The mansion was huge, and even having spent my childhood here, I doubted I knew every nook and cranny. Hell, Gil had this place remodeled so often, sometimes I wondered if it might as well be considered a whole new building.

We both had our way of dealing with our past, and our murderous father. I had killed him and run. She had stayed and rebuilt.

So I kept walking and then I thought of a place. One place I knew she would not change.

I found my father's study right where I had left it all those years ago. The place I had come to associate with magic. This was where our dad had told us about our heritage and terrified the living daylights out of us with a demonstration of power. This was where he would assess our progress.

This was also the place my mind projected when my magic was locked away. It was in a mental version of this space that I had fought Wrath and won (with a little help from a certain love-preaching angel). This was where I had unlocked my magic and made peace with the whole thing.

Entering the study, I felt calm. I had faced this fear and overcome it. The place was dusty and smelled like old books. Most of the volumes here were historical. Family diaries, written by those who came before my father, but way after the Ashendale name had ceased to be one of the big leagues. Most of them were whackos and despots, little more than raving lunatics with visions of grandeur.

Gil had left them here in the dust.

The couch, once a dark maroon, now a disgusting blend of dark splotches, was caked in dust and mothballs. The cozy chair was turned toward the fireplace. My father had liked sitting there, usually with a brandy hanging over the side and a book on his lap. Now it was empty and vacant.

I wondered why Gil had left this place like this.

"She must have been looking for something."

The voice startled me. I turned, hand on the hilt of my sword. The wizened Chinese man before me looked anywhere between sixty and six hundred, even though I knew he was much older than that. On this occasion he wore a silver Chinese suit, matching his beard and storm-grey eyes.

Sun Tzu approached and ran a finger over the back of the cozy chair.

"I am not reading your mind, Erik Ashendale," he said, eyes twinkling with humor. "But I do know you well enough to guess what is on it."

He clasped my shoulder with one hand. "It is good to see you, my friend."

There was a time when I would have hugged him or shaken his hand. That was until I had learnt who—or what

—Sun Tzu really was. An Avatar. A portion of that entity we call God.

And the four emissaries he had with him—Turtle, Long, Phoenix, and Tiger—were also a part of him. If Turtle was involved in something, it was only a matter of time before this guy came out to play.

"You are troubled," he said.

"What do you want?" I asked.

Sun Tzu gave me a withering glare. "No."

"No, what?"

"No, you do not get to act like a sniveling child just because you are hurting, Erik Ashendale," he said. "You are better than that."

I sighed. Sun Tzu was a father figure to me. In a way he had helped shape me into a decent human being.

"Sorry," I said. "But I don't think I can handle any more bad news."

"The demon will pull through," he said. "His part is not yet over. In fact, it has yet to begin."

He gestured towards the couch as he pulled out the cozy chair. Dust and mold and god-knows-what-else disappeared when he lowered himself on it. I sat on the couch and found it was clean. It was the same as when I was a kid.

No, I had to remind myself. Things changed. I had grown up.

"On this occasion I do not present you with bad news," Sun Tzu said. "In fact, it is time."

"Time for what?"

"For you to know," he said. "You have questions. You have had them for a very long time. Now you are ready for the answers."

With a wave of his hand, the fireplace lit up. Purple flames swirled and grew, turning blue as they reached us.

They consumed the world around me, enveloping the study in blue fire. Maybe Sun Tzu had seen the vileness of this place and was going to burn it down.

When I opened my eyes, I was surprised to see myself still sitting down, with Sun Tzu still on that cozy chair just like my actual father would have been.

But the study had gotten a lot bigger. Multiple couches occupied the newly created space, and the beings sitting on them were anything but human.

Sitting closest to Sun Tzu was an old woman with black holes for eyes. Her teeth were fangs and she had a necklace of eyeballs around her neck. Two licks of flame hung over her shoulder, obscuring some of her facial features in shadow.

Next to her was also a woman, but one that looked like the supernatural version of Two-Face. Half her face was that of a stunning blonde, the other half was utterly zombified. This parallel ran all the way down her body, even in her clothes. The right half of her tunic was beautiful stitched leather—the left had rotted away to shreds revealing decayed flesh beneath.

The biggest being that had appeared was an elephant man. Literally—an elephant sitting like a man wearing a bright red-and-yellow tunic, with a series of earrings on his massive Dumbo ears and waving a thick-fingered hand at me that could have crushed my entire upper body. He leaned over and said something to the creature next to him.

This one was a talking tree—a tree with massive reindeer horns and cloven feet, which shook loose evergreen leaves every time he moved. He was smoking from a long pipe which he passed to his neighbor:

A humanoid jaguar.

There was a god on fire, who looked like an overweight

man at the beach, complete with the wide-brimmed hat and towel, except for being completely on fire.

Next to him were two gods that could have passed for twins—if they had been separated at birth and one raised by the upper class and the other in a cave. The upper-class one I recognized from the stories.

Zeus was tall and proud, wearing a pristine white suit, and his face was like a moving storm cloud. Lightning would occasionally zap along his face.

His twin was thicker and stockier, wearing little armor over his white tunic, and had a beard twice the size of his head. It was wide and unkempt, and where Zeus's lightning was tame and controlled, like electricity conduits, this guy was wild and sprayed bolts all over the place. He grinned at me and rolled his eyes at his twin's direction. I liked him.

Next to him were two gods I also recognized. Aten was easy to guess by the falcon head, and Mahees was an actual lion with bizarre human facial features. He was also made entirely out of gold.

The final two were the creepiest. The woman, Kali, had a million arms and it made me nauseous trying to keep track of all of them. Her legs were long, shapely and bare, and she was practically daring me to peek under her dress.

I knew better.

Barely.

The one directly next to me on the couch had four pairs of eyes, and a mouth that opened like a spider's, complete with pincers. His dark skin glimmered in the light of the fireplace, and that was when I noticed his suit was made entirely out of cobwebs. He grinned at me like a used-car salesman, and that told me I was sitting next to Anansi, the Story-weaver.

"Welcome, Erik Ashendale," Sun Tzu said. "To the Council of Deities."

There were a lot of grunts and murmurs (Hekate, the first goddess, winked at me, and Kali made a sound that I usually associated with the female orgasm—both gestures equally unsettling).

"Is it time yet?" asked the elephant man. Ganesh—that was his name.

Sun Tzu nodded. "It is our turn to provide direction."

Jaguar growled.

"No, we do not hunt yet," Sun Tzu replied.

"But soon," Mahees added. "I can smell it in the air. I can smell it on the mortal."

"Cease your smelling, then," Anansi said. He draped an arm over me. "This human has such a story to tell."

"Is that all you ever care about?" Zeus's twin asked, in the thickest Russian accent I've ever heard. "Story, story, story. Every time you tell story, I lose will to live."

Hela, the Norse half-zombie goddess of the underworld, turned to glance at him.

The god looked down embarrassed. "Um... I not mean literally." He winked at me again. "Vikings. No sense of humor. You, mortal. You know who I am?"

I shrugged and looked at Sun Tzu before answering. The latter nodded.

It was never safe to reply to a god.

"I don't," I admitted. "I know who your brother is."

The god exploded with lightning. "BROTHER? This idiot is not my brother. He is my copy. A cheap, *weak* imitation."

"Hold your tongue, Perun," Zeus said. "At least I have value. What do you bring?"

"I bring power!" More lightning exploded from Perun's

face. "I bring thunder and lightning. I bring storm to break Earth. While you chase woman by turning into swan. Like sissy!"

"Enough!" Aten snapped. His voice had a screeching raptor-like quality to it. He turned to Sun Tzu. "We have business to attend. Let us be done here."

"Not yet, honored Aten," Sun Tzu said. "Unlike us, this mortal requires words."

"Oh, I like words," Anansi said.

"Silence," snapped Kali.

I turned to Sun Tzu. "What's going on?"

"Banter," he replied. "Gods are easily bored. And more easily distracted."

Oh good. The upper echelon of deities had a serious case of ADD.

No wonder the world has gone to shit.

"The threat comes," said Ganesh. His voice was weirdly smooth and silky. "The Calamity is approaching."

"A creature capable of initiating the end of the world," said Anansi. "Apocalypse, death and destruction. The kind of thing that would make the Great Fall look like an opening act."

"The Great Fall?" I asked.

"Anansi," Sun Tzu said. "You should learn to hold your tongue."

Jaguar roared.

"Oh hush, you," Anansi said. "We keep spinning the mortal in circles."

"Because we do not know what will happen if we tell him," Sun Tzu said. "Once we tell him about the Calamity he will go looking for it. *That* could very well be the catalyst that unleashes it."

"I'm right here," I said.

The gods ignored me.

"Its arrival is foretold in many tales," Anansi said. "If the human can kill it before it is ready then we may… Human?"

I had stood up and was walking away.

"Oh, I'm sorry," I said sarcastically, turning towards them. "I was just leaving."

"Why?" Ganesh asked.

"Because this is useless," I said. "You're not going to tell me anything, and quite frankly, I'm not sure you can."

I sat back down regardless.

"Because here's the thing," I said. "For all your power and knowledge and all that shit, your people still suffer. Now that you have a chance to take your thumbs out of your mouths and actually be useful, you sit around arguing whether I should know something or not.

"The thing is, I've faced a million calamities," I went on. "Everything from Lilith, all the way to the Underworld last year. Shit kept piling on, and yet we survived. *Without* you. So please, feel free to keep talking amongst yourselves. I'm gonna go and actually be useful."

For a long moment no one spoke. I tensed myself, ready for someone to leap at me. I had basically just called a whole group of gods useless—better get ready for the smiting and lightning.

Perun threw his head back and gave a thunderous laugh.

"I like him. This one has the *balls*!" he roared at Sun Tzu. "You make good choice."

Then he turned to me and it was like being in the middle of a storm. "You want me talk to you? Okay, I talk to you now. You don't know shit. You need someone to point you in right direction. Calamity or not, you have problem, *now*."

"The Vault," I said.

He nodded. "The Vault. You must find it. Greede say he know. He does not. He is liar who buy time. The longer he have Sword of Michael, the stronger he get and more options he have. So you must hurry. Find the Vault."

"Okay, where is it?"

"Do I look like god of knowledge to you? Pay attention, stupid. You need to find the right source. If you want to find a place, what do you need?"

I shrugged. "A map?"

"Very well," Ganesh said, actually applauding. "I thought it would take more nudging. You are not as dim as your species lends us to believe."

I chose to ignore the compliment-insult combination and instead focused on Perun, the one eager to talk.

"Where is the map?" I asked.

"Where you keep all maps," he said, shrugging.

So much for useful.

"Okay," I said. "Any more takers? Anyone got a suggestion where I can find this map?"

"Have you considered a library?" Anansi suggested. "They got plenty."

"Right. A library. So which library would have the map to the Vault?"

"Wrong again," Perun snapped. "You don't actually need map. You need knowledge of map. So find knowledge."

"Show of hands who is a god of knowledge here?" I asked around the room.

Kali started raising a few of her hands before grinning and retracting her arms. "No, not the kind you seek," she explained.

Something clicked.

Knowledge. Thoughts.

"Hey, Sun Tzu," I said, "is the map inside the mental realm?"

Sun Tzu smiled and nodded.

Ganesh applauded me again.

"Yes, yes, more clapping," Perun said. "Give ribbon to intelligent monkey."

"Indeed," Aten said. "The realm your progeny resides in is the location you must go to. There you shall speak to one of *my* pantheon." He hesitated. "He is of the older generation. He may prove... difficult."

He said it in the exact same way as "Parents, man. Can't live with 'em; can't live without 'em."

"Okay," I said, nodding. "This is progress. Go to the mental realm, find the library, locate the map, find the Vault, kill a Sin, come back in time to watch the game. Sounds like a plan."

"Beware, Erik Ashendale," Sun Tzu said. I could sense he wanted to say more but couldn't. "There is mortal peril ahead."

I shrugged. "What else is new?"

Then looking at Zeus in particular, I said, "Can we count on you for the Aegis when the time comes?"

The god nodded. "When the time comes."

The tree god, Cernunnos, spoke for the first time. "My Druid hath already secured the Lighting God's trust. Thou would do well not to question it, Warlock."

"Can't help to double-check, can it?" I shot back. Then softer, "And thank you. I appreciate Emrys' help, and yours, with the Spear of the Sun."

"Speak not of things thoust doth not comprehend," he said.

But there was none of the snappiness from before. Indeed, he went back to contentedly smoking. Maybe the god of nature needed some acknowledgement from time to time.

Everyone likes to feel appreciated.

"Erik Ashendale," Sun Tzu said. "We must leave now. Fellow brethren, I thank you for your attendance. We shall meet shortly."

"Good luck," Perun said. "Try not to die."

Before I could come up with a good retort, Sun Tzu snapped his fingers. Purple and blue flames consumed us again and once more we were sitting alone in the study.

"That was... trippy," I said.

Sun Tzu shook his head. "Must you antagonize everyone you meet? It is a good thing they found you amusing, and not offensive."

I shrugged. "I spoke the truth."

"Truth hurts," Sun Tzu said. "Especially to those of higher power. These are beings of fragile egos."

"Well, it's about time someone kicked them in the balls then. The universe is at stake, and all our lives along with it."

"Perhaps," he said. "But it would be best not to anger them. You would not like it if they kicked back."

I chose not to respond to the challenge. Truth be told, they could atomize me, sure, but maybe not. I was powerful, and I had faced beings that called themselves gods before.

And from what I could tell, I was supposed to face this Calamity which had them all shitting their pants.

But arguing with gods was futile. Best move on and get things done.

"Right," I told him. "We need to get to the mental realm. Can you secure us a ride?"

He nodded.

"Good," I said standing up. "I'll assemble a team. Wheels up in ten."

16

As soon as I entered the meeting room again, Turtle stood up. He gave me a nod and walked past me.

"It is in your hands now, Erik Ashendale," he said as he walked by.

"What is he talking about?" Abi asked.

"The Vault," I said. "I know where it is."

Greede cocked his head. "*I* know where it is."

"You don't."

"Yes, I do."

"Well, an actual god told me you don't," I retorted.

Emrys turned his gaze towards Greede. "You said you knew," he said. "Did you lie to me, Greede?"

I snickered. "No shit he lied to you."

"Now, wait a second," Greede protested. "I know where the Vault is! I also know how to get there. Why did you think I wanted your sister here and not you? She knows how to operate the portals inside this place, and *that* is how we are going to the library."

"The library that contains the map which will lead us to

the Vault," I said. "Ergo, you don't actually know the Vault's location."

"And where is this map?" Greg asked.

I shot Greede a look, non-verbally inviting him to answer.

The latter sighed.

"In another realm. One made of pure thought." He looked down. "I was hoping Gil Ashendale would have a better understanding of it and know how to lead us there. I understand she has conducted experiments before."

I frowned. Okay, so Gil was playing mad scientist again. File that under 'To Be Dealt with Later'.

Provided we actually got her back.

Emrys shot Greede a vile look. "I think it's time we reconsidered the terms of your release, Mr. Greede."

"I know how to get us there," I said, changing the subject back to the topic at hand. "I... um... have a way in."

Abi cocked her head. I wordlessly asked her not to make a scene. Not yet at least.

Mothers can be touchy about their kids.

"And Turtle's leader—I suppose we could call him that—offered to help with the traveling as well," I added. Sun Tzu had offered a ride but I wasn't sure how far that favor would extend. Then again, the gods seemed desperate enough to get us on this mission, so I was thinking that I could get them to play ball.

"Our mission is the library," I said. "In the Mental Realm. There is a school we have access to which can serve as a back door. Gil's got portals here—that means a way in and out. You, asshole!"

Greede looked up.

"Can you operate the portals?"

He nodded.

"Good. We have our tech man."

"I should go too," Greede said. "I can safely navigate the Mental Realm."

"How so?"

"Willpower, and years of discipline."

I glanced at Emrys.

"You stay," the Druid said. "We can discuss certain things while Erik is gone." Then undertone, "Like how many teeth you get to keep."

I wordlessly thanked him. You see, the last place I wanted Greede was where my kid was.

I have a child.

With Abi.

But this is no regular child. Oh, no, nothing in my life is ever that simple. Our child was a thought-form, a psychic entity named Zeke.

Most of the time Zeke—presumably along with a host of similar beings—resided in the mental realm, enrolled in a school run by Sun Tzu to teach them how to better control their powers. Think of it as the supernatural version of the *X-Men* without the snazzy outfits.

Either way, Zeke was my child and I loved them (non-binary plurals for the being that was both feminine and masculine, often at the same time). They'd offered to help me multiple times, but still, I felt kind of shitty asking my child for help. Especially when there was this much danger involved.

And if Greede ever found out... I shuddered to think to what lengths he'd go to in order to use Zeke against me and Abi.

"I need someone else," I said.

Abi was about to volunteer when I shook my head. I couldn't have her around me, not in a place where every emotion was literally visible. We would light up the place and all notions of stealth would go out the window.

"I will go," Greg offered. "I have entered the realm once. It was not pleasant but I can hold my own."

I nodded at him. "Any other takers?"

"I can't spare anymore, Erik," Emrys said. "Not for a retrieval mission. We have work to do here."

At his nod, the rest of the Grigori dispersed from the room.

"What kind of work?" I asked.

"The kind that will save our lives once you get back with the map." He grabbed Greede by the arm. "On your feet, you."

"Good luck, Mr. Ashendale," Greede said as he was escorted out.

That left me, Greg and Abi. The Kresnik took a look between us and hastily left.

"Zeke is your way in," Abi said. Her voice was calm. Never a good sign.

"Sun Tzu hinted as much, yes," I said. "Look Abi, I don't like this as much as…"

"You keep our child away from danger, Erik," she interrupted.

"Of course," I said.

"Good. Keep them safe and away from all this," she went on. A tear streaked down her face. "You know, Amaymon wasn't just your family, Erik. We all feel the loss. We're grieving, too."

"Only I was the monumental ass," I said.

She flicked a strand of red hair away from her shoulder. "Yes, you were," she said matter-of-factly. "And just so you know, we need to have a good long talk about what you said in front of Anael." She jabbed her finger into my chest. "But you take care, and you be careful, and whatever you do, you come back. Understood?"

"Yes, ma-"

She leaned in and kissed me suddenly, retreating before my brain had a chance to catch up. I stood there reeling for what seemed like minutes. I mean, could you blame me? One minute she was slapping me and storming off madly, the next she was kissing me...

Women. Number one cause of mortality in men.

I was starting to get why.

We had to get naked, Greg and I, and stand on the sigil marked on the floor.

Nudity was not something I am shy about but this was a frigid room with an icy floor and a spectator's box—the Grigori insisted on watching us depart and keeping an eye on Greede, who was calibrating our destination and wolf-whistling in our direction.

I flipped him off. Greg ignored him.

Hey, there can only be one mature guy. Them's the rules.

"Why the fuck does it have to be so cold," I grumbled.

Greg had shed off everything and handed his spear to Emrys. Physical weapons were useless where we were going. I had done the same with Djinn and my gun.

"Is okay," he said. "Not too bad."

"Yeah but you grew up in Siberia," I told him.

Greg shrugged his shoulders which on a six-foot-plus naked guy made a lot of things shake loose. Including a bit I could not help but glance at. I mean, it made sense. Greg was a big guy, and everything was in proportion. Of course, that just made things worse when I remembered this guy was dating my sister.

"You are looking," he commented, keeping his gaze forwards, but grinning slightly.

The bastard.

"Whatever. Ring any doorbells with that thing lately?" I shot back. "Actually, don't answer that. I don't want to know what you and Gil get up to."

"That is probably for best." He chuckled. "You remember when you threatened to castrate me?"

"Yeah."

"Good thing you carry a sword, then."

I sighed.

Luckily, the sigil went off at that moment, and Greede yelled, "It's time. Close your eyes. You'll feel like falling in three, two... one..."

And the world was pulled from beneath us.

When the sensation of plummeting down an abyss with no end finally subsided, I opened my eyes to a bizarre world.

I had been in the mental realm before, but no matter how many times I saw it, it was always strange. The world was blueish, with translucent accents where *things* usually went in our world. Instead of a sidewalk, a building, or a streetlamp, the thought world had tall, or thin, or short, or stocky blobs that all represented a thought pattern associated with the thing they were supposed to be. So instead of a table, you had the thought of a table.

Confusing?

I know.

I looked down and saw myself as a blueish blob with a lot of black trapped inside, like someone had messed up a glass-blowing project. The blackness inside me was writhing and streaming along the edges, threatening to get out.

A few of the Thought-Forms that passed us, all blueish or purplish humanoids, paused to glance at me before walking on.

Greg appeared beside me, a humanoid of blue and royal purple, accented with white. He too was looking himself over.

"This is very strange."

I didn't have time to think about a good retort when one of the doors opened and a familiar Thought-Form ploughed straight into me, wrapping delicate yet surprisingly strong arms around my waist.

"Father!"

17

Zeke got their hugging strength from their mother apparently. Either that, or the school they attended had a mandatory weight-lifting program, because the kid was strong.

Rib-crushing strong.

I patted the kid on the head until they released me and I gave Zeke a hug. I would have been content to remain like that for a few hours, hugging my child.

But we couldn't.

Not yet. Not with an apocalypse hanging on the horizon.

Zeke stepped back and looked at Greg. "Nice to meet you, sir. You must be Greg."

The latter raised an eyebrow in my direction. "Pleasure to meet you as well," he told Zeke. "I have no idea who you are, little one."

"Zeke," they replied. "I am named after an angel."

"I see."

Zeke turned and shooed away a stray strand of purple that emanated from another child-like entity. "No. This is private."

The entity went away, sulking.

"You have to be strict with some of them," Zeke said. "They do like to pry." They frowned at me. "But first I must disguise you, Father. You look rather sinister."

I looked at my hands. Shadows swirled visibly beneath my blueish glowing skin.

"Stand still, please," Zeke said. They caressed the air from top to bottom, their hand slowly dropping. I felt magic coalesce with that movement, encasing me.

When I looked down, the shadows were gone. I could still feel them, but they simply weren't visible. A reddish tinge instead occupied their place.

"There," Zeke said. "Now people will think you are merely angry."

"Not different from real Erik," Greg interjected.

"Yeah, I wonder why that is," I retorted. "Sister missing, girlfriend angry, demons rising, angels hunting me down, Amaymon in a tank..."

I trailed off, suddenly aware that Zeke was staring at me.

"Did mother finally speak to you about her issue?"

"What issue?" I asked.

"Never mind."

Oh great. Even the kid was secretive now.

"It will all be good, Father," Zeke said, sliding their delicate hand into mine. My hand was three times the size of theirs. It was weird hearing Zeke speak like an adult but knowing they were less than a year old (technically speaking), and that as a thought-form age meant nothing to them.

"Now we must go see the headmaster," they said. "He is expecting you both."

Zeke led us ahead. Traveling in the mental realm is always a bizarre experience. For one thing, there is no actual floor. Concepts like force, motion, acceleration are all gone.

You moved by willing yourself forward. It wasn't like spatial magic either, where you folded space around you and warped your body to another physical location. Over here you simply thought of going forward and you did.

Greg and I warbled a little, me more initially, before we hit a particularly nasty bend where Greg skidded into a wall, and Zeke had to pull him back. It amazed me to watch the kid. I mean, they'd been here for about a year, and already they were navigating the mental realm like fish navigate water. And that spell... Zeke could rarely interact with the physical world without major distress to them. But here he had just disguised my body like it was nothing, pulling off an illusion even his mother would have been impressed by.

The world around us shifted. There were more humanoid thought-forms now—other students I presumed—and the building we entered narrowed. The corridors were tighter, and there were more doorways.

A school, I realized. *The* school.

Zeke stopped in front of a pair of double doors that were in stark contrast to everything else we had seen.

For one thing, they were solid. I mean actually solid. Possibly the only solid, material thing in this whole universe. For another, they were made out of gold and bore two door handles in the shape of twisting Chinese dragons.

Zeke paused and politely knocked once. The dragon handle on the right hissed at them, before spinning on itself and leaning forwards. The door opened and Zeke smiled at us, beckoning us in.

As we approached, we became more solid. I felt my feet hit solid ground and my spine stiffened as actual weight settled on my skeleton. It was me, I realized. My muscles, my clothes, even my hair—I felt every ounce for an instant before my brain readjusted to being physically whole again.

Greg examined his hands and scanned the office. It was a spartan, wooden affair, with a large desk largely devoid of any paper, computers, wired gadgets, or indeed anything you might think belonged on a desk. Two chairs, not dissimilar from what you might find at a doctor's waiting area, sat in front of the desk.

The singular man behind the desk was standing up with his back to us. He wore an ivory suit that had strands of actual starlight woven into it. Long white hair reached the nape of his neck.

He turned.

Sun Tzu had gained a couple of pounds of pure muscle. I had always known him as the frail old man who looked like a good gust of wind might topple him over. This version was a few years younger. His skin was a healthy shade of tan, his wrinkles were almost nonexistent, and his beard was neatly clipped to a point. Only his serene smile and storm-grey eyes remained.

"Welcome, Erik Ashendale. Welcome, Greg, esteemed Kresnik. I trust your journey was not too discomforting."

He motioned for us to sit down, while Zeke hovered behind me. Sun Tzu glanced over at me and nodded with appreciation.

"Excellent craftsmanship, Zeke."

I could feel the kid beaming from behind me. Hell, I could *see* their happiness radiate in pulses of blue.

"Thank you, Mr. Longfang," they said.

"You are dismissed. Please wait outside while I speak to our guests for a moment."

"Yes, sir."

Zeke spun on their heels like a soldier and exited the room. I raised an eyebrow at Sun Tzu.

"You have questions," he said.

"Oh, where do I start," I said. "One: since when does *my* kid have that much respect for authority? Two: what's with the suit, man? Three: did you discover an anti-aging potion? You know, like Keanu Reeves. And Four: Longfang? Really?"

Greg looked incredulously at me.

"What?" I said. "He asked."

Sun Tzu chuckled. It was still the same laugh. That made me feel slightly more at ease.

"Well, young Zeke is a prodigy in this school, my friend," he said. "I daresay they have inherited both their parents' talents for magic, quick-thinking, resourcefulness…" He paused and smiled. "And for locating trouble."

"There we go."

"However, where you lacked a father figure and the proper guidance, Zeke has more than enough people here who are willing to listen to them and nurture their considerable talents."

I tried really hard to suppress the pang of envy. I mean, does that make me a bad parent if I felt envious of my kid?

My father had left a literal demon to educate us (and I'll give you three guesses to how nurturing that had been), then he had tried to kill us, forcing me to run away. Then I had met Tenzin, the kindest man I've ever had the pleasure of meeting, who had helped keep me sane and on the right path—before he was killed in my arms.

Actually it's a wonder I'm doing as well as I am.

"How I appear in this realm is more accurate to my actual representation," Sun Tzu went on. "And that includes my moniker. It is truer to my truest self."

"You got that from a fortune cookie, didn't you?"

Sun Tzu sighed. "And I do not know this Reeves man you speak of. Is he the one from those robot movies you tried to introduce me to?"

"*Terminator*? No, that's Arnold Schwarzenegger. This guy is from those *John Wick* movies."

"The one with the guns and the dog?"

"Yep."

"Most implausible."

"It's a movie! And when this is over, I'm also making you watch *The Matrix.*"

"I like the movies," Greg interjected. When I raised my eyebrow at him, he shrugged. "What, I felt left out. And movies are fun."

"Gil's not a fan, is she?"

"She enjoys Netflix and... how you say... chill?"

"Dude! That's my sister!"

"I am sorry."

"Do you even know what that means?"

"No," he said, genuinely confused. "Because she always interrupts the viewing with sexual-"

"Okay!" I said. "I'll explain it later. Back to the issue please, before I lose the will to live."

"Perhaps that is for the best," Sun Tzu said. "You are here to access the Library."

The way he said it made it sound like it should have a capital 'L'.

"In there you will find the only map that will accurately lead you to the Vault," he went on. "However, you will have to barter knowledge."

"What sort of knowledge?" Greg asked.

"I do not know," Sun Tzu admitted. "The Librarian, Mr. Thought, is rather... difficult. Eccentric, one might say. He may just let you pass without incident, or he may set his beasts upon you."

"A librarian with beasts," I said. "Great. And what kind of name is Mr. Thought. Little on the nose, isn't it?"

"It is the Egyptian god of knowledge, Erik," Greg said. "Thoth."

Sun Tzu glared at him. "Refrain from mentioning that name, please. The librarian seeks knowledge wherever he can find it and I have many secrets I wish to keep until such time as I choose to reveal them."

"Sorry," Greg said.

"Wait," I said. "You're saying that a god is guarding your library? Who wants access to all forms of knowledge?"

"Yes," Sun Tzu said.

"Would this help?" I fished out the laminated key card that Anael had fashioned for me so we could access the gateway to Heaven. "It's a key to Heaven."

Sun Tzu pondered for a while. "I see. Yes, that may be payment enough."

"Excellent," I said. "So just point us in the right direction and we'll be off."

"Zeke will take you," Sun Tzu said. "They certainly spend enough time down there."

Once again I shook my head. My kid, the bookworm. Guess some of my sister's genes had popped up, too.

As we got up to leave, Sun Tzu held up his hand.

"One final thing, and this is of the utmost importance, Erik: do *not*, under any circumstance, allow the Librarian to find out you are an Ashendale. He is obsessed with warlocks, and your bloodline especially."

"Why?" I asked.

"I do not know," he admitted. "But what I do know is that if he does find out, you shall never leave that Library for as long as you draw breath. So stay under Zeke's illusion, and whatever you do, do not attract attention to yourself."

18

"Wow."

My soft exclamation resounded like a stick of dynamite going off in an echo chamber. A thousand studious individuals looked up at me from their books and collectively shushed me.

"Father," Zeke said. Their voice did not echo, I noticed. "Please do not draw attention to yourself."

Great. Chided by my kid.

Sorry, I mouthed.

Again half a dozen angry heads turned at me. I realized that my *sorry* thought had taken shape and floated away, a blob of purple energy. Zeke extended his arm and quickly caught it before it could travel any further. With a flick of his wrist he dispersed the thought.

"Listen only, Father," he said. "Do not speak, and do not respond. Simply accept my words without comment."

Greg chuckled. His voice did not echo. How were they doing that?

"You are asking the impossible, young child," he said.

"He will try his best," Zeke said.

I balled my fists but I had to stay silent while the other two talked about me as if I was a pet they had to lug around. I considered flipping them off, but no parent should flip off their child no matter how well-merited the gesture was.

See, I can be mature.

Zeke led us ahead, deeper in between stacks of books and towering bookshelves of all sorts. Some were square and boxy, others spiraling around a staircase, others still built into a variety of polyhedrons with ladders jutting out. Some students were upside down, climbing ladders that jutted out from the ceiling towards the floor, but they didn't seem to mind.

What's more, this part of the Library, like Sun Tzu's office, was physical, too. At least the floor was. Parts of it melded into the mental realm, so you had the longer bookshelves that would start with wood at the bottom and finish semi-opaque at the top.

Zeke took us down a spiral staircase that became darker as we sank deeper below ground. The smell of must and old books entered my nostrils, followed by the stench of extremely strong disinfectant which still could not hide away the metallic tang of blood.

Trust me, I can recognize that scent anywhere.

This Thoth guy was up to no good.

Another set of doors greeted us, these ones black and shimmering as if they couldn't make up their mind whether to stay solid or turn into liquid. They swung open without Zeke even raising a hand, and in we went, into a room filled with even more books.

And scrolls. And sheaves of loose paper. And what looked like tablets made of stone and clay stacked into haphazard piles.

And little silver discs that brought back memories of the

Vensir, a race of humanoids that I had rescued from a pocket universe created by the Sin of Envy.

Long, *long* story.

Basically, this was a repository of knowledge, both human and otherwise.

One of the laptops—there were about fifty of them all crammed on some desks—beeped. A man with wild black hair and a burgundy robe ran out, waving about a slight reed which I recognized as a stylus, the original writing implement.

Thoth waved a pattern over the computer and let out a chuckle. Then, as if sensing our presence, he turned with the sort of erratic neck movement usually found in birds.

Which wasn't far off from what his face looked like.

It was as if someone had totally messed up the graphics on a video game character. His face was elongated and tipped at the nose, which hung curved until it went past his upper lip. His eyes were orbs of swirling silver light flecked with gold.

When he walked, he shuffled forward with a hunch and I saw that his arms were very ape-like, with long, delicate, spidery fingers curling from thick knuckles and strong wrists.

"Zeke," he said. His voice was quiet, like a drop of water echoing in a cold dark cave. He turned his eyes towards me and Greg. "And guests."

"Mr. Longfang sent us down here, Mr. Thoth," Zeke said. "These gentlemen have need of your knowledge."

Thoth shuffled in closer. His nose was flexible, not quite elephantine but certainly more than a regular human's would be. Not that a regular human nose hung down like that.

"A Kresnik," he said, examining Greg, before it was my

turn. "And a human. Something is wrong with you, human. Are you a magician?"

I frowned. "Um, yeah, I guess. We go by wizard now."

Thoth threw his head back and laughed. It was like hearing ice shatter.

"Wizard. From the root word 'wisdom'," he said. "My my, the hubris of man knows no bounds. You consider yourself wise, mortal?"

"I have my moments," I said. "Few as they may be."

"Are they?"

"Very."

"Good," Thoth said. "At least you are smart enough not to lie to me. I despise liars. This is why I delighted so in killing the King's court magicians. I gave them power, taught them the first arcane words, but they soon forgot whom they should worship."

He absentmindedly tapped a key on the laptop. It didn't seem to like it so it beeped back. Thoth kept tapping, seemingly deaf to the machine's complaints.

"I was of the first generation, the god of the moon and all of its wisdom. I gave man the first roadmap, the first shelter, the first midnight ritual, and sheltered him from all things dark, showing him how to turn death into life. I showed him how to build and ignite, I instructed him in ways of knowledge to better survive. And look where it got me: they turned my serene visage into that of a monster's, renounced the moon in favor of the sun, and embraced their own foibles. But I showed them. I invented the scientific disciplines to counter the magic I had taught them, and ensured that science prevailed with a vengeance. Thus ensuring that all magic-users face retribution throughout the centuries."

I gulped.

All those witches and wizards, sorcerers and practitioners—all those lives lost throughout the centuries where fearful men hunted down those with special abilities.

It was all this guy's fault.

Now it clicked why he was down here, and Aten was up there. Thoth was in exile, serving out a punishment of some sort.

Good.

I hoped there was an afternoon evisceration I could witness. This guy sure as hell deserved it.

"What it is you seek?" he asked.

"A map," Greg answered. "To the Vault containing the demon Belphegor, and the Sin of Sloth."

"Ah, yes," Thoth said. He stroked his stubble which was in patches. "Written by the Grigori. But are you not one of them?"

"Our memory has also failed us," Greg said. "The knowledge was lost due to countless acts of treachery."

Thoth sighed theatrically.

"Humans. You will lose your own heads were they not attached to your necks. And sometimes you manage to lose them still!" He chuckled villainously. "I do have the map, of course. Do you have something of equal import to trade?"

"How much do you know about angels?" I asked him.

Thoth looked at me like I was a centipede crapping on his favorite pillow. I like that look—it usually meant they were either about to say something incriminating, or they were going to show off and give me what I need to hear.

Either way, win-win.

You know, provided they only spoke and not threw lightning bolts at me or something.

"More than they care to admit," he said. "And certainly plenty more than you mortals know."

"But not enough, correct?" I said. I flashed the laminated card.

The way Thoth looked at it, you would have thought I presented him with his own fantasy island, a private jet, and couple extra million just for kicks.

"Where did you come by that?" he asked.

I pulled it slightly back. His eyes widened even more.

"An archangel made it for me."

"Anael. I recognize her signature," he said. "You will give it to me."

"Upon your word that you will trade us the map for it," I said.

"No," Thoth said. "The map cannot be removed from here. It is the last of its kind. But you can look at it and take pictures." He pointed at a stack in the corner. It was full of ancient cameras. "No flash photography, please."

"That's okay," I said, pulling out my cellphone. Miraculously it was still intact. "I brought my own."

Thoth nodded. "Excellent. Hand over the item, please." He extended one wide spidery palm.

I placed the card on it. He tucked it away with glee.

"Just out of curiosity, how will you get there?" I asked.

"Never mind that," he said slyly. "I have my ways."

Of course you do.

Thoth beckoned us forwards. If you thought the foyer of the library was cluttered, then get ready for Hoarder Central. Thoth collected everything. And I mean *everything*.

You had your standard books next to figurines, next to a stack of computers from WWII onwards, next to a bucket of keys ranging from key cards to those old unwieldy affairs they used in the Dark Ages, presumably to unlock a castle or something. CDs were piled in a small mountain to the right. Candy wrappers to the left formed a stouter, if wider, mountain. Weapons were tossed haphazardly inside a series of chests, swords mixed with flintlocks, revolvers of all eras, Luger pistols with Roman shields, spears (both broken and not) joined by obsidian and flint arrowheads.

Then, we got to the ancient studies room. I assumed it was ancient studies, because a massive series of Greco-Roman statues greeted us, along with the Greek ones, the Celtic ones (hey, Cernunnos statue), and finally the Egyptians. I noticed that most of those were vandalized and their heads broken.

(Aten had a large chunk missing in the crotch area. Guess Thoth was petty like that.)

Then came the maps.

And holy kittens were there maps.

If I lived for another thousand years, I would not have been able to go through all of them. Not that I would spend my theoretical additional years looking at maps—that would be cruel and unusual punishment.

They were stacked so high they formed a maze. Thoth led us through and finally pointed at a section.

A section as wide as a wall, and twice as long, covered entirely in rolled-up scrolls.

"This section," he said. "That part over there is the latest. Work your way back."

Without so much as a goodbye he spun on his heels and left.

Greg sighed and rubbed his forehead. "I will start here," he said pulling out a handful of scrolls. "Here, you take these."

"If I may, Father," Zeke said. "I can help."

The kid stood in front of a section to the far left, spread their arms, and a faint blue light emanated. Their essence sometimes flickered as they speed-read.

But even with Zeke's amazing ability, and Greg's seemingly endless patience, we had a lot of scrolls to go through.

I grunted and picked up the first from the pile Greg had given me.

Cruel and unusual indeed.

19

We could have been down there for half an hour or a million years. That should give you an idea of how long it felt. I like books, and I love reading—give me a crackling fire and a fantasy novel any day—but this was just mind-numbing, eye-watering labor that made me grumble about setting things on fire.

Zeke laughed and kept speed-reading. Greg, on the other hand, looked apprehensively at the exit.

My neck complained. I massaged it, groaned, and hatefully looked at the map on the table before me. I closed my eyes and heard something flapping.

I looked around. Greg was still reading, Zeke motionless.

Flap, flap, flap.

"Guys, do you hear something?" I asked.

Greg looked up, blinking rapidly, and frowned. "What?"

"Listen," I said, raising my head to silence him.

More flapping.

"Don't you hear that?"

"Sounds like book," Greg said. He shrugged. "We are in library."

"I must agree with Greg, Father," Zeke said. "It seems that-"

Fwoom!

A book slammed into my face, flattening my nose, with page corners snapping against my eyes. I flailed in what I can only assume was a manly and totally non-cartoonish way, and clawed at the psychotic volume.

The book deadened as soon as I had it in my hands, and sat quietly.

The volume was about the size of a pocketbook, like one of those small Bibles you find in hotel rooms. That was pretty much the only similarity.

The title in front of the dark, stained leather cover read WYRLOGA in dull gold capitals.

I recognized the title. It was one I had seen in a library much smaller than this, on an island that was populated not by people but by a race of humanoids called the Vensir. An island created by the Sin of Envy, Leviathan.

An island my ancestors had visited once, and this book spoke of them. I had glimpsed it on my way inside the Vensir library while looking for a way to get off the island.

Magic surged through me.

When I blinked away the light, I was no longer inside the Library. Not unless the Library had decided to pick that moment for some refurbishment and become an exact replica of my inner world.

Ashura was a red place, with red sands, and a red sky. You would think it was a warm place, like some rocky mountain deserts, but nope. It was utterly devoid of temperature. It wasn't hot, nor cold, winds did not exist here, much less blow and howl, and moisture was nonexistent. It was just *there*.

In the middle of the desert stood a giant black tree, with

roots canopying the base. Each was about as thick as my waist, mangroves that were all too familiar to me. I half-expected to see the avatar of my curse power, Dark Erik, but I had absorbed him into me not too long ago.

No more avatars.

Just a talking tree.

"Not time yet."

I glared at the tree. "Oh, come on. We've been doing this dance for eight years. Just tell me what you are."

"I am you." Typical. *"Yet also not."*

"Yeah, thanks, real useful."

A pause.

"When?" I yelled at the tree.

"Soon. Find your other half. The book is the missing piece."

What?

I racked my brain. Other half—Gil! I had to find Gil.

"Yes," the tree said, showing that unnerving ability to read my mind. Then again, it was my inner world. There were no secrets here—just withholding information apparently.

"Wait for her return. When she speaks of a missing piece, give her the book. Thus the map is complete."

Another map? Seriously?

"Seriously, Erik Ashendale. The place you are in is a map to all things. That very much includes the Ashendale Legacy."

"What legacy?" I'd heard this story before. Supposedly there was a massive... something... that my ancestors had buried beneath their land.

And by land I mean a whole island they erected from the seabed.

Now what was left of it was the Ashendale estate. That is, the mansion and lands around it.

"Find the other half. Deliver the final piece. Take your Legacy. You are close, Erik Ashendale. You are ready."

And with that final, completely not ominous statement, Ashura ejected me back to the real world.

Well, the Library.

I looked up and saw Zeke's concerned face.

"Father?"

"I'm here, kid," I said. The book was still in my hand. I thought about opening it and leafing through, but something told me that would be a bad idea.

Look at me listening to my instincts and playing it safe.

"YOU!"

Thoth appeared at the entrance. His robe was open, revealing a loincloth beneath (thankfully).

"That book!" he screeched, pointing at the volume in my hands. "That book is mine! Give it back."

Instinctively the book took flight again and wriggled into my coat, digging itself into a pocket.

"I guess it doesn't agree," I told him. "Look I didn't do any-"

"THIEVES!

The map room melted and I felt as if someone had grasped me with a fishhook and yanked me across space and time. When the room stopped spinning, we were in the foyer again.

An alarm went off in the distance.

Every person there, the people who had shushed me, stood up. Blue blobs turned into angry purple. Guess being pissed off came color-coded in the mental realm.

"An Ashendale!" Thoth said imperiously. He was on the balcony and pointing at us.

I looked down. Shit, he was right. Zeke's illusion must have shorted out when the book took me to Ashura. I was there with my ass hanging out—spiritually speaking of course.

Over here I did not have an ass.

"Long have I waited to exact vengeance upon you," Thoth said. "Your clan is a cancer on Earth."

"That was like a billion years ago, buddy," I said. "Get with the times."

"Everybody out!"

The blobs disappeared leaving us alone with a very pissed-off long-faced god.

Two massive shutters clanged open and the heavy sound of thick chains being unlocked echoed through the Library.

"I don't suppose Thoth is known for keeping really big and cuddly kittens, is he?" I asked.

The other two rolled their eyes at me. Zeke chuckled derisively.

Yeah. It's never kittens.

Two beasts the size of SUVs came thundering through, knocking aside tables and shelves, trampling on books and scrolls and everything else.

They walked on four legs, which were thick and heavy like an elephant's, and had razor-tipped trunks. The similarities ended there. Their feet were razor-clawed, and a massive sail rose from their backs, along with a series of porcupine quills each as long as a jouster's lance. Sleek tails with fins on them undulated left and right, giving the creatures balance.

From their heads, thick clomping jaws with a single massive tooth from one end to the other, like a massive wall of enamel, emerged. They looked like beaver teeth—if the teeth were size of climbing spikes.

Finally, from their skulls emerged four horns, each as long as my whole arm. You would think they would be top-heavy, but the beasts charged unfettered, swinging their horns at anything that stood in their way.

"Behold my Set Beasts," Thoth cried, raising his arms like a cheesy villain. "Kill them, my lovelies. Kill the thieves and heretics!"

20

In my experience, when shit hits the fan, life becomes real simple: either you're the one who freezes or the one who leaps into action.

Or at least that was what I thought until recently.

Until I had a child.

Until that same child was in the room with me.

I did what I was trained to do, what I would always do: I leapt forward, only this time in protection of a being that I had conceived, that I loved beyond any reason or sanity, a single individual for whom I would burn the world...

Only Zeke was faster.

They winked out of existence and reappeared a few inches in front of me, hands outstretched, and a blast of energy erupted. It slammed into the Set beasts like a wall and threw them backwards. One of them was already staggering back to its feet.

Zeke swayed and I caught them.

"What was that?" I asked.

"Buying us time," they replied. "For that..."

Greg swung a spear of pure white light at the first Set beast and gored its side. The beast struck the shaft with a tusk and ripped it away. Greg summoned a second one out of thin air.

I pulled Zeke aside and hid them in a corner. "You stay here, kid," I said. "No matter what, you stay here and be safe."

"Father, I can…"

"No!" I had to swallow hard. There was something in my throat. "No. Zeke, you need to stay safe. I need to know that. Stay here."

They nodded.

I stood up. "Greg, I need a weapon!"

"Cannot," he yelled back. "Is holy magic. You have bad reaction."

I swore.

"Erik, you *are* weapon," he said. "Look at you. This is mental realm. Use your head."

Before I could contemplate what he fully meant, the second Set beast leapt for me…

No, for Zeke.

I roared and thrust myself at it. The black energy inside of me exploded through my arms, wrapping around my fingers as I in turn wrapped them around the beast's legs and held on. The Set beast turned to me and I did the only thing I could think of.

I head-butted it.

Energy swirled around my forehead, creating a long tusk that emerged and gored the beast, and the impact sent it flying.

Use your head.

Never say I don't take advice literally.

Still, I wasn't going to get another shot like that. I needed my tools, my weapons. I wasn't even sure my magic would work here.

The Set beast swung at me. I held out my hands defensively and heard the clang of a shield being struck. The impact sent me off my feet but I was still in one piece, while the shield that I found myself suddenly holding evaporated away.

"Okay," I said. "Let's try something sharper."

This was the mental realm. Thoughts were real. You think it, and if you can fully back it up, it would be made manifest.

I held out my hands and closed them around imaginary hilts. The same hilt I had held since I was a kid, the weapon that travelled with me everywhere I went.

A pair of Djinn replicas appeared in my hands. I grinned.

"Round two, tusk-face."

I dodged beneath the tusks and blocked the second pair. Bits of ivory flew off. Magic surged through my feet, planting me on the ground and giving me purchase. I heaved. The tusks slid off with a jarring, teeth-clenching noise. The beast's neck became exposed for a second. I struck, burying the blade of my right sword into its neck and slashing. Thick fur absorbed most of the impact but I hit flesh. Thick gooey ectoplasm seeped through the wound and the beast retreated.

I glanced backwards. Zeke was gone, winked out of existence. I didn't have much time to think about where they could have gone because the beast was back on me and this time it was pissed.

Yeah, well, so was I.

Both my swords turned into energy and I blasted the beast with them as it charged. The Set monster staggered and veered to the left. I reached up and found a handful of fur I could use to climb over its neck. It reared backwards in an attempt to throw me off. A thick cord of obsidian energy wrapped around its neck like a garrote, linking the ends to my hands.

I started pulling.

The beast screeched and screamed and raged, but I had my strength and the energy rope bit into its flesh, cleaving through fur, then hide. More ectoplasm spurted out. The beast toppled sideways but it wasn't dead yet.

I held myself firmly on the ground and kept pulling.

The Set monster's head came rolling off and a blast of released power snapped into the room like a shockwave. I staggered. The beast's carcass was turning into ectoplasm.

Something hit me in the shoulder. Thoth was screaming at me but thanks to the ringing in my ears I could not hear him. I did however see his hand light up with green energy as a lance of power shot at me.

Black shadows emerged from my shoulder, deflecting the bolt from where it would have hit.

"Should have gone for the head," I said.

I held out my right hand. Energy started building up, first blue and purple, then black. An oily pitch-black, darker than tar, that kept piling on and on. I shaped it conically, like a lance, and held it up.

The lance was easily the size of a Humvee, and aimed straight at Thoth. The god looked at me with eyes wide open.

Greg yelled. His spear thrust missed and one of his Set beast's tusks ripped through his side. It was a shallow wound but I saw it in slow motion: how the next tusk would gore him. Greg was tough and I've seen him recover from some serious damage, but I wasn't taking the chance.

I adjusted my aim and threw the lance of black power towards the Set beast.

The explosion rocked the whole world. Parts of the Library ripped away, turning into ectoplasm and blue energy that dispersed into particles. The Set beast was dust. Greg was slammed backwards and slumped on the ground, bleeding from the head.

I ran towards him, just as Thoth emerged from a pile of rubble. His hands were glowing.

"Erik, don't!" Greg said. "Look at yourself."

I looked down and saw myself covered in shadows. They were bubbling and boiling, lashing out, eager to be released. I had little doubt I could take on Thoth even if he was a god —but at what cost?

I could already feel myself losing control. It had been years since that had happened. It had to be because I was in the mental realm. There were fewer filters here.

If I wanted destruction, I could have my fill of it here with almost no cost—except that the destruction would also apply to me.

The *me* that made me human.

Like I said, no filters.

So I focused on shielding Greg and deflecting Thoth's energy beams as I grabbed the Kresnik and hauled him towards the doors. When I pushed them I saw Zeke on the other side.

"No! Thieves! Thieves!" Thoth shot more energy but he couldn't get past my writhing shadows to get a clean hit, and there was too much rubble for him to easily reach us.

We passed through the door and Zeke shut it behind us. Thoth banged on it but the door never opened.

"He cannot cross over," Zeke explained. "It is part of his punishment."

Greg found his feet and rubbed his head. "Well, that could have gone better."

I looked down at myself. The shadows had retreated back inside me. I turned to Zeke.

"Where did you go?"

"To the map room," they said. "The task was to find the location of the Vault. I did that with little distraction while you were fighting."

"You... you..." I took a deep breath before pulling them in for a tight embrace. "You stupid idiot. I told you to stay safe."

"But I was safe, Father," Zeke said. Their arms were light around me, yet I felt their strength. They smiled at me. "You were handling the bad guys. I found the information. Divide and conquer."

Greg chuckled. "Too smart to be your child, Erik."

I swatted him on the shoulder. "That's Abi's influence," I replied.

Zeke grinned. It was a little disconcerting. Their teeth were a bluer shade of blue than their face. My eyes were having trouble adjusting to the weird color spectrum of this place.

They leaned up and told me where the Vault was located.

"You're shitting me!" The phrase escaped my lips before remembering you should not swear in front of children. Zeke didn't seem to notice.

"What?" Greg asked.

I told him. He raised his eyebrows in the non-verbal equivalent of my exclamation.

"Well, good thing you like snow," I told him.

Greg grimaced. "Yes. But this might be too much snow. Thank you, Zeke. You were very brave."

Zeke nodded. "You too, Greg. And you, Father." They smiled. "But you must return to your realm now. It is no longer safe for you to be here. Your physical bodies will degrade and I'm afraid that will be especially bad for you, Father."

They were right. The shadows were itching to escape their confines.

"Will you be alright?" I asked, glancing at the Library doors.

Zeke chuckled. "Thoth is just throwing a tantrum. Mr. Longfang—our version of Sun Tzu—warned him that he would be receiving visitors today and to cooperate, but he still insisted on being petty. He will calm down in a few hours. Perhaps I will play a board game with him. He does like that."

I patted the little warlock book in my coat pocket. It was still there, intact and tiny and a whole lot more trouble than I had asked for.

"Come, Father," Zeke said grabbing my hand. "Time to say goodbye."

"You take care, you hear?" I said, hugging them again. I kissed the top of their head.

We stood there for what seemed like too little time before we parted.

"You tell Sun Tzu or whatever he goes by here that he better keep his promise to look after you," I said.

Zeke nodded. "I am sure he knows, Father. As does Thoth. I am safe here." They seemed to glow. "I am happy."

A sigil formed beneath the ground where Greg and I were standing—the beginnings of a teleportation spell. I felt that familiar sensation of being sucked into a void.

"Oh, and Father," Zeke added. "Do speak to Mother. She needs you more than you think. Promise me."

I opened my mouth but I no longer had one. I was just a mass of atoms being separated and sucked through the portal. Everything went black and when I opened my eyes, I was back inside the Ashendale mansion.

21

Coffee.

Whatever your problem, however urgent it is, coffee should precede it. It's not just the act of drinking—it's a hot beverage that, unless you want to scald the inside of your mouth, will make you slow down. Stop for a moment, analyze the situation.

That was the first thing I did once we were back at the mansion. I headed off to an empty room while Greg went with the other Grigori and we did our separate versions of winding down. Abi came in with a cup and sat down.

"How is Zeke?" she asked.

I looked up from the cup. "Our kid is awesome. They seem happy. Though they need to work on facial expressions."

Abi scoffed and chuckled and took a seat next to me.

The room was a dining hall of sorts and one of the new additions. Thick curtains prevented the brunt of the afternoon sun from coming in. Judging from the unused furniture, unblemished floors, and slightly discolored surroundings, I would say this room had never been formally used. Maybe it was next on Gil's 'to be torn down' list.

I was sitting on one of the chairs, which were not the most comfortable, but I was happy to have something solid against my body. Abi pulled the chair next to mine. We both stared at the curtains and the corona of sunlight brushing around their edges.

"How are you?" she asked.

"Weird," I said.

"Tell me something I don't know."

I snorted. "Traveling to that place is always…"

"Weird?" she supplied.

"Yep."

"I could never go there," she said.

Not everyone is built to travel across dimensions. Hell, only reason I can do it is my unique magic. The other Grigori have a crap-ton of power so they can withstand it.

But most wizard-level magic users are Earth-bound. Which is not a bad thing most of the time. I've been to Hell (literally), Heaven, a pocket universe, a Limbo dimension, and now the mental realm—let me be the first to tell you Earth is amazing. It's where we should be. It's where coffee, books, and family are.

It's *home*.

Unless one of that family happens to not be there. Then it's a bummer.

"You and Zeke still speaking psychically?" I asked.

She nodded. "We can both astral-project, so I visit them in school sometimes." She smiled and I knew she was fighting to hold back a tear. "But I miss the hugs."

I hesitated but then wrapped an arm around her. She could elbow me in the face if she needed to.

She didn't. Abi leaned into me and sobbed softly.

"I'm sorry for being an ass," I said. "Turns out everyone knew I was due for some ass-time... wait, that didn't come out right."

Abi burst out laughing. "This is a serious moment. Don't bring asses into it."

"Hey, I am what I am."

"No shit, Sherlock," she said, straightening up. "And I probably wasn't exactly upfront with you about something..."

She stood up and paced. Uh-oh. Abi only paced when things were real bad. I'm the pacer in this relationship. I'm the chaos, she's the anchor.

"It's my succubus powers," she began.

My mind went racing. Abi is beautiful, hot, smoking—whatever you want to call it—and a big part of that allure is her demonic heritage. She could look in any direction and make guys crawl towards her. And girls, too. Pretty much everyone wanted to bang my girlfriend, and while that is a very egocentric point of pride for my male brain, it is also a source of concern. Not that Abi ever did anything to make me doubt her faithfulness to our relationship.

Ever.

"It's not that," she said, frowning at me. "I would never do that."

"Well... I mean, you can't blame me for thinking that," I said.

"I suppose not," she replied. "But my concern is about you and me, Erik. That maybe you got used to my power. Maybe you let your guard down. Maybe..." She sighed. "I know we talked about this already. But sometimes I fear that you're with me because of *what* I am."

I looked at her in silence.

"And don't give me that look," she snapped. "Look, I

know it could all just be in my head, but things are changing fast and I'm not your apprentice anymore, which means... I don't know what it means. And we're together now, and I love being with you—I love you, Erik—and we have Zeke and it's... It's just all too much."

She sat down, deflated.

I started laughing. I didn't mean to, but it suddenly felt like a massive weight had been lifted off my shoulders.

"Hey!" she snapped. "What's wrong with you?"

"Nothing," I said in between hiccups. "Look, Abi, you're just human. You freaked out. And why shouldn't you? Our lives are a chaotic clusterfuck of demons, angels, crazy wizards, talking cats, and now we have a kid who has more in common with *Casper the Friendly Ghost* than with us."

I set down the mug and took her hands. She squeezed my fingers.

"We're messed up," I went on, "but don't you ever doubt how much I love you. And I mean *you*, the person. Yeah, the package is nice, and yes, the succubus side is sexy as hell—but none of that means anything without you being you."

Her lips pursed into a smile. It was adorable and oh-so-sexy.

"You know, you're not so bad with the words," she said.

Our lips met, sending a fresh wave of fluttery, happy emotions into my system.

"We should have had this talk," I said in between kissing, "sooner."

"Yeah. Now shut up and kiss me."

I did.

We stood up, hands roaming. Fear, adrenaline, anger, and pretty much every other emotion I felt melted away into lust and passion, and I was very okay with that.

I kissed her neck. Her shirt came off. Mine followed

soon after. She turned. I kissed her neck and collarbone, and she made a noise that made my pants a few sizes too small.

They came off too, and soon the room was filled with the sweaty, sloppy grunting of passionate lovemaking.

Most action that dining room had ever seen.

22

"Well, someone is happy," Greede said, as he sipped on a chai latte from Starbucks. "You two look positively sinful."

Abi and I both raised our eyebrows in unison at him. Then I knocked away his cup.

"Hey!"

I grabbed him by the collar, shook him, then threw him back in his seat. "I don't want you getting comfortable here, Greede. I want you stressed and on your toes the whole time."

Abi glared at him. "And no more comments."

Greede said nothing. She looked almost disappointed.

"Well," Emrys said, "if we are quite done."

He spread his hands over the topographical map in front of him.

I nodded and went ahead and grabbed some doughnuts. I offered one to Abi who grinned at me.

We were both hungry.

I mentally high-fived myself.

"Go ahead," I said. "Did Greg tell you which slice of paradise we're visiting next?"

"Da," Greg said. "Antarctica. Coldest place on planet Earth."

"Antarctica?" Abi echoed. "As in, we-haven't-discovered-a-lot-of-it, glaciers-are-melting-fast, no-civilization Antarctica?"

"Yep," I said, through a mouthful of bear claw. "Sweet, sweet ice and snow. Hey, do you think that's where Led Zeppelin got the idea for that song?"

Emrys gave me a look. "It is one of—if not *the most*—inhospitable places on our world."

"Gee, sounds terrible."

They all shot me a look.

"What?" I said. "Look, we've been to Heaven where practically every angel wanted us dead, I've been through Hell under the same circumstances, and Greg and I just had words with a literal god. Somehow I can't bring myself to be scared of some ice. We'll pack heavy coats and lots of food. Oh, and maybe one of those dog sled thingies. I've always wanted to ride one of those."

"Is fun," Greg commented. "Just do not fall. Then is not so fun."

"Is there a way we can portal through?" Greede asked. "I for one am not too keen on frostbite. And your powers, Druid, will be rather limited in a place where vegetation is weak. That makes two carriers of the Keys vulnerable." He nodded to no one in particular. "I see the brilliance of placing the Vault there. The climate itself is already crippling, and who knows what other challenges we are sure to face."

"Don't assume you know anything about my powers,

Greede," Emrys snapped, but I could tell from the way his eyes were on the map that he was worried.

Druids were supposed to be extinct until Emrys had showed up. From what I could gather, only a sparse handful remained, and practically nothing was known about their powers—only that they paled in comparison to the Druids of old.

"We can't portal in, can we?" Abi asked. "Because we don't have a ley line to anchor with. Because we don't know the place."

Emrys shook his head. "There is one," he said. "Right here, straight down the middle. It follows magnetic south, as opposed to true south."

I sighed.

That meant that the closer we got to the magnetic pole, the more unstable our magic would become. Which ruled out using magic to force our way through, or even sneak in reliably. We would have to march straight at the Vault and knock on the front door.

Emrys seemed to be thinking along the same lines as me.

"According to our research, using the Earth's magnetic field was the only way to safely contain Belphegor," he said. "Now that he has the Sin awakened in him, that is also the only thing keeping it held inside the Vault."

"Which means options are limited," Greg said. "We must take straight route."

"I agree," I said. "But we'll be vulnerable. Never mind the climate—if I were to put something that dangerous inside an ice box, I'm gonna make damn sure said ice box is protected from nosy travelers."

"Like us," Abi said.

"We will need an expedition," Emrys said. "A full army."

"No," Abi told him. "Gil's forces are not trained for that sort of environment."

He smiled at her.

"Oh, I am aware of that. But I wasn't thinking of *human* troops. Greg, contact Evans. Tell him Winter Soldier is a go. I will need as many of them as he can spare."

Greg stood up and picked up his spear. "I will lead them. I know my way around that kind of terrain."

"Excellent. Meanwhile, I will inform the rest of the Grigori. We will need the whole squad to mobilize."

Greg left and Emrys turned to me and Abi.

"I assume you are ready to depart."

Abi nodded. I grinned.

"What about me?" Greede demanded.

Emrys bore an icy stare at him. "What about you?"

"How do you intend to transport me?" Greede asked. "How will you endeavor to keep me alive now that I am a key member of the expedition?"

"You can walk like the rest of us," Emrys said. "You'll wear thermal clothing at all times and keep yourself hydrated and well-fed. You will also not stray from us."

"Of course," Greede said. "I promise."

"Yeah, like I'm going to take your word for it. Seneschal!"

The chair Greede was sitting on suddenly melted, letting the guy fall on his ass and hurriedly scramble back up.

The chair took the shape of a translucent, watery humanoid, and a familiar yellow raincoat flared out. One of Seneschal's arms had not formed—instead it was a mass of goo that was still wrapped around Greede like a straitjacket.

"Seneschal will be your security detail," Emrys explained.

Greede regarded the creature before him. "A Polymorphic Bionoid," he observed. "With sentience too. Can you do magic?"

Seneschal remained quiet. Honestly, I wasn't even sure he *could* speak.

"Strong and silent type, then?" Greede said. "Those make the best help. Curious, though. You look like one of Renakaten's creatures. However did you escape his thrall? He was a remarkable alchemist, one of the best in the world."

At the mention of his creator, Seneschal raised his left arm. The opaque flesh rippled and a long scalpel-like blade replaced his limb. He pressed it threateningly against Greede's face.

Emrys barked something that sounded vaguely German—maybe Teutonic, or High Germanic; I was never a language guy—and Seneschal froze midway to giving Greede a new facelift.

The blade melted away and from the mass holding tight onto Greede a tendril of opaque liquid flesh wrapped around Greede's mouth, silencing him.

I nodded appreciatively at Seneschal. His blank face rippled, forming a wide, creepy smile, and he gave me a thumbs-up. Then he frog-marched a protesting Greede out of the room.

"I like him," I said.

"Gil thought so, too," Emrys said. "He's fiercely loyal to her. We think she's the first person to ever treat him like… you know… an actual person. Greede will have a tough time breaking through him."

I opened my mouth but he sighed and said,

"I know. And we're handling it. Just be ready for when it all hits the fan."

"Always am," I said.

Emrys gave us one final nod and left, taking the map with him.

"I need to talk to you," I told Abi as soon as we were alone. "But not here. Follow me."

I took her out of the room, outside of the whole wing actually, and we went towards where Amaymon was being held.

The room was empty, the only light coming from the glowing green liquid which held my familiar's demonic feline form suspended. A few wires had been attached to him, leading to machines and consoles around the circumference of the tank. I wasn't able to accurately read them but I didn't need to. The ruby pendant was still cracked and he was still out of it. That was information plenty.

"Sorry to spring this up on you," I told her, "but I need to know. Abi, do you trust me?"

She frowned at me. "What do you mean? Why are you asking me that?"

I could see the confusion in her eyes. I knew Abi loved me, no question about that. But trust is different. You can love someone and not fully trust them. You can earn trust and it's one of the hardest things to do ever. Find someone you love and trust and you got yourself someone truly special. Someone you can be open and vulnerable with. Someone you can share a life with.

Someone you can ask tough things of and know they will do the right thing.

I needed Abi to make a choice—a final choice when it came down to it—and one that was made a thousand times harder *because* she loved me.

"I do," she said, meaning it. "Is this about Antarctica? Are you leaving me behind again?"

I nodded.

"Is it to protect me?" she asked. "Because I told you, Erik, I don't need that-"

"It's not that," I interrupted. "But there's something I can only trust you to do. Did you look into that thing I asked about right before we left for Jehudiel's mission?"

She frowned then nodded. "Project Ic-"

"Not here," I said. "Don't mention the name. We know how paranoid my sister is. The place is likely bugged."

I looked around and then back at her. I handed her an earpiece.

"Take this. When I give you the signal, set it off."

"What?"

"Set it off." I swallowed the lump in my throat. "On my coordinates."

Her eyes widened. "Erik... no... If I do that, you're all dead."

"It's the nuclear option," I said, "but it needs to be in play, given what we are facing."

"No," she said. Her voice was pleading now. "No, there has to be another way."

"I'll survive it."

"Bullshit! You don't know that. Your sister designed it specifically for something like the Knightmare! You!"

"Abi, listen to me!" I seized her hand. She didn't fight me. I planted my other hand on Amaymon's tank.

"We need to do this," I said firmly. "We need this on the table and I only trust you with it. I am trusting you with my life. With *saving* my life."

A single tear ran down her cheek. "You'll die."

"No, I won't," I said. "I have you to come back to, and

Zeke needs me to be the dad mine wasn't. I intend to stick around to make you happy."

"Please, Erik..."

"I'm too stubborn to die," I told her. "You know that. And this guy—" I tapped Amaymon's tank, hoping for a reaction I did not get "—is too annoying to die. So face it, woman, you're stuck with us for a long time."

Her hand shook as she took the earpiece but she kept her face steady and strong.

She always made the right decision no matter how hard it was.

God, I loved this woman.

"You better come back," she said. "You hear?"

Without waiting for my response, she leaned in and kissed me something fierce.

"You better goddamn come back," she said.

"Yes, ma'am."

And by God did I mean it.

23

Question: how do you get an expedition to Antarctica?

Answer: you get your rich friends to hire a boat.

Given that we were all what amounted to a bunch of freaks—and psychos in Greede's case—it wasn't as if we could just make our way on any research boat. Any contact with civilians was prohibited, especially with a prisoner as dangerous as ours, so instead we had to find a decommissioned research vessel, fix it up, and have it sail-worthy in the span of a few days.

They got the job done in thirty-six hours. I didn't know whether to be impressed most by the magic or the money.

The ship was large enough to accommodate all of us, plus a crew of twenty Australians and a literal boatload of equipment for navigation both on sea and on land, survival, and most importantly, a lot of weapons.

Unlike conventional charter flights or cruises, our destination was a little more remote. We couldn't just portal to south Argentina, pay a captain, and off we go. For one thing, the furthest our portal could extend was Brazil. The Ashendale records showed that there *had* once been a magical road to the closest South American port to Antarctica but it had been destroyed.

Seems like someone really did not want us there.

Also, given the Vault's approximate location, traveling from Australia was better.

So there we were, in the company of Rocco, a liaison for the Grigori, with tan skin, perfect abs, blonde Bodhi-from-*Point-Break* hair, piercing sea-green eyes, and an attitude that was all smiles and grins and subtle flirting.

I hated him on sight.

The journey there was mostly uneventful. We all kept to our quarters. I roomed with Greg and Emrys, who had different ideas of comfortable. Greg slept with his spear, caressing the weapon like a freaking teddy bear. Emrys has a routine of applying balms and natural oils to his skin before going to bed. I made fun of him—he made pollen fall on my pillow while I was sleeping which resulted in an hour-long sneezing fit.

Evans took the cargo hold, along with about twenty heavy-duty boxes, like the type the army uses to transport missiles, while Greede was in the farthest and smallest room we could shove him into, along with Seneschal for whom space was not an issue. He never once let go of Greede, either wrapping a tendril of his opaque flesh around his ankle, or binding both his arms. Greede didn't try anything

I mean I did press him over the railing before we left and threatened to take him to Antarctica as an ice sculpture.

On day two, Rocco met us at the mess (it's the dining room for all you non-boaty people) and announced we would be entering a really dangerous fissure that had been heavily affected by global warming. Emrys also suggested that this glacier weakening meant that the ley lines holding the Vault secure had weakened—hence our predicament.

We knifed along, ice on all sides. The cold was... indescribable.

It wasn't just cold. It was soul-shredding, gut-wrenching, bone-shattering cold. The only approximation I had was the third circle of hell, Cocytus, which I had journeyed to once. At least in that place, the cold affected you according to how much of a prisoner you were. I had been exempt from that.

Not from this.

This was officially worse than Hell.

I went outside wearing my coat and what could only be described as a whole bear's worth of fur on top of that. Massive glaciers loomed over us on both sides, going as far as the eye could see. They weren't simply big—they were world-consuming, covering everything from sea to sky. Once we cleared them, I had to put on goggles that offered extra protection from the sun. As the sun beams reflected on the ice, the sunlight became blinding and extremely hot, like when sun beams reflect off a mirror.

Except the mirror was everywhere and also ball-bustlingly cold.

Finally, the ship came to a halt and we made our descent. I was the first one down, heavy, hob-nailed boots crunching on the snow and sleet. We were each armed to the teeth, and not just with magical gear. I had a compact rifle that looked more like a toy than a weapon. Several ammo clips were belted next to my handgun. We all carried flares and a radio, as well as a few food packs, enough to keep us alive for a couple of days if we got lost.

Rocco and his crew opted to come along with us as an armed escort. Emrys said they could be trusted. Judging from the way Rocco was holding that rifle, I was ready to bet he had never fired a single shot in his life. Hell, I would bet he had never fired a single *spell* in his life at anyone. Still, maybe we were going to get lucky and a polar bear would eat him first.

Occasionally Emrys would stop our march, take his glove off and bury his arm to the elbow beneath the frost. He would stay there for a few minutes, eyes closed and in complete silence.

"Up ahead," he said when he did this for the third time. "There's a base we can use for shelter."

"How far are we from the Vault?" I asked when I reached him.

"Don't know," he replied. "It's two days walk straight ahead for sure. Then we just hone in on the signal and-"

"AAAHHHHH!"

We all turned in the direction of the scream. One of Rocco's men was on the ground. His leg was missing. There was blood all over the snow, staining it in a pool of red that instantly congealed.

His leg was two feet away from him, ripped by something jagged and pointy.

"Move, move," I yelled as I pushed my way through.

Emrys knelt by the injured man while I tied a tourniquet around his stump.

"What happened?" I asked.

"We don't know," Rocco said. His eyes were wide and he kept looking around as if expecting something to jump out. "One minute he was there, I think he was trying to warm himself up with magic, and the next he's on the ground missing a leg."

I heard the ripping before I heard the scream. When I turned, another man was on the ground but he wasn't bleeding. It was one of Evans's golems. It was a woman who screamed, another of Rocco's crew.

"Shit," I said. "Everyone, form up."

We all huddled together into one massive group, guns pointed outwards at the endless snow.

"No magic," Emrys yelled. "I think whatever this is, it's attracted by magic."

"No magic?" Rocco cried. "Sod this, mate, I'm outta here."

"Rocco, no, don't use magic!"

But it was too late for my warning. Rocco broke formation and took two steps forward, and a pair of jaws erupted from beneath the ice and clamped around his throat. Rocco went face down, blood shot all over the spot, and the creature sank back.

"Shit! Everyone start moving," I said. "We need to get clear of open snow. Emrys?"

"Three minutes at two o'clock, there's a big rock that can fit all of us," he said. "But we will need air support."

"On it," Luke said.

He was the only one of us without a weapon. With one deft movement he shed his thick jacket, showing he was wearing nothing beneath, and set himself ablaze.

The ice rumbled but whatever leapt out at him could not catch him before he shot into the air. I spotted the creature.

It was a wolf made entirely out of jagged ice. Sunlight reflected off the crystals on its back. It was easily the size of a polar bear, with a set of jaws almost as big as its whole head.

Luke sent a blaze of fire down at it, and the wolf yelped. It sank into the ice with a sizzle and plenty of steam.

I heard more growling and spun. The gun rocked in my

hands, pumping lead into the spot where just a second later an icy wolf head emerged.

"Move, move, move!" I cried.

We fired at our surroundings, aiming for the slight ripples in the ice which indicated the wolves were leaping out. I hit several of them but more kept coming.

Luke flew overhead and set one on fire. The beast yelped and roared, but down into the ice it went and came back up in one piece.

"It's the crystals," Emrys yelled over gunfire. "They are reflecting the heat. Just like the rest of the ice here."

"Then we must attack them with melee weapons," Greg said. He tossed his rifle at one of the golems, who caught it and dual-wielded the weapons like they weighed nothing. Greg pulled out his spear and let it shine with something other than just reflected sunlight.

"Emrys, change of plans," I said, holding my rifle with my left hand as I pulled out Djinn. "You lead, we distract."

Emrys nodded.

"Mustafa," he cried.

"Here," answered the mustachioed Grigori.

"We need cover."

"Will do."

To his credit, Mustafa handed his rifle to one of his pretty—and now I could see, also deadly—assistants, and set to work creating an Abjuration barrier that would mask the party. It wouldn't completely hide them, but that was where Greg and I came in. We were the distraction.

"Niamh, Morgana," Emrys cried out. "Flank the party. Usher back any stragglers."

The two fey women split up. Unlike us, they did not require any special clothing, and were much faster.

I stopped running and turned. Greg was about ten feet

away, his spear held at the ready. The ground beneath us rumbled and warped.

"Come on, come on, come on, COME ON!"

I roared and ran forward, towards the wolves, firing my rifle without pause. Bullets shattered the crystals on the nearest one and kept digging until blood spurted out. I reloaded but couldn't bring my weapon to bear. Instead I dodged and channeled magic into Djinn. The blue blade sliced through the crystals and flesh beneath.

Greg roared from the side. His spear was faster than lightning, and he was raking up a death toll that left a small pile of lupine corpses behind him.

One of the wolves clamped a jaw around my right arm. Teeth began sinking into the flesh but I had plenty of clothing on. I shoved my rifle into its mouth and let off. Bullets flew from behind its head, hitting the ones behind it.

Greg and I kept pushing through them, our magic attracting more and more. From my peripheral vision I could no longer see the party. Even Luke had descended into the barrier.

But I could still hear gunfire.

Suddenly a whole bunch of golems came through, big expressionless men wearing arctic jackets and wielding guns. They ploughed through the line of wolves.

Roaring a battle cry, I threw myself back into the fray, cutting, slashing, and fighting. My rifle clicked empty one more time, and I put it away without reloading, leaving it dangling from a strap. Using just Djinn, I got close and personal. Shadows grew from me as I called my magic.

Let them come.

I hacked and slashed. Magic seeped from me, exploding upon contact, tearing through the enemy ranks.

But there's a reason you don't bring explosives to icy

places. You see, we were still on that precarious piece of land, still navigating past the fissure that was oh-so-delicate.

Ice doesn't care about heat (unless it's global), or about guns, or bombs for that matter.

It cares about vibration and pressure.

And boy were we making a lot of noise.

I heard the cracking like a roll of thunder. I even looked up because that was what I associate that sort of sound with. But it came from below, and then Greg was yelling at me, charging at me, pushing me away, as the ground beneath my feet gave way, and suddenly we were falling…

And falling…

24

I woke up screaming. My entire body felt on fire, like a thousand daggers had decided to take residence inside me. Icy daggers. With barbs and thoughts of revenge.

"Easy, easy," came Greg's voice. The man himself loomed over me and adjusted the small mountain of coats and furs piled on top of me. "You took great fall. Frostbite. Your body is healing but you need to not move."

"What happened?" I asked.

"The ice broke," he said. "We all took a great fall. You were buried beneath it for several hours."

"Hours? Dammit, how long was I out?"

Greg shook his head and kept stirring at something that vaguely smelled like tea. Either that or I had a seriously weird concussion that made ice smell like dried herbs in boiling water.

"Hard to tell," he said. "Perhaps two or three hours. We have been inside this cave for two more."

I swore again.

So that meant five hours of no communication with the

team, five hours of distance inside this frozen wasteland, and five hours of daylight gone.

"How long until sundown?"

"Forget about it, Erik," he said. Greg came over and handed me a cup of tea. It was one of those you unscrew from a thermos cap. The tea was flavorless but warm, and my insides came alive for one brief moment before the muscle cramps started. "You cannot traverse land in your condition. Even healthy men will not do it in the dark." He huffed and looked outside. "We must wait for morning. Emrys and rest will be at camp by now. They will take shelter there."

"Any communication?" I asked.

"Spells not work well here," he said. "Not with magnetic interference. Anything psychic is out of question. Emrys can send familiar but creature he thralls will die in the cold of the night. It is futile attempt and waste of energy."

I nodded. Yeah, he was right. We needed to preserve every ounce of magic we had until we reached the Vault. No sense in putting ourselves in dire conditions just to hold off a few minor enemies.

If only someone could have listened to his own advice a few hours ago.

"What happened to the golems?" I asked. "These are their jackets I'm buried under."

Slowly I managed to sit up. The cave Greg had found was tiny and completely buried under the ice. A small opening barely large enough for one of us to crawl out of was at one side, held open by small rocks. Djinn was stabbed in the middle of the doorway, along with several assault rifles that were starting to freeze over.

"What's with that?" I asked.

"Magic sword will not freeze," Greg said. "It will provide

a space to get stones out and open door. Otherwise snow will bury us alive. But other weapons..."

He pointed to the side.

My gun, rifle, along with his spear and a few small handguns, were all disassembled and partially wrapped in a blanket. Already I could see the beginning of frost burn on the barrel of my rifle.

"We lost all golems," Greg said. "Some ice crushed, others malfunctioned when cold interfered with internal systems. Even Evans's magic cannot endure long under these conditions."

"So we're on our own," I said.

Suddenly I had this urge to hide under the blankets and not come out. Instead, I said,

"Do we know at least where to go once morning comes?"

Greg nodded. "Yes, I memorized route. We need to take shortcut through valley."

"Why do I sense trepidation?"

"Because valley is uncharted."

"Well, fuck me with an icicle," I spat. "Trap?"

Greg shrugged. "Maybe. Or maybe there are things in this place we not yet discovered. Could be civilization."

"Oh sure, cos that usually works out well for both parties," I said sarcastically. "Either they honor us as gods and sacrifice us to release us from our fleshy confines, or they try to and we kill them first."

"You watch too many movies," Greg said. "We will not end up like pirate of Caribbean."

I frowned at him. "You said you never watched those."

"Gil enjoyed them. She likes comedies. And I like when she laughs."

I made a retching sound.

"Oh, please," he said, "like you and Abi are subtle. Or Luke and his boyfriend."

"Jack," I said. "He was a student of mine for a short while. Never knew he played for the other team though."

"Neither did he," Greg said. "Until, according to Luke, he became enamored by certain sword-wielding Wizard who saved him from life of poverty."

Despite the neck cramps, I managed to turn my stunned expression towards Greg.

"Say what?"

Greg chuckled and finished his tea. "You never wondered why Luke looks at you like enemy?"

"I figured it had something to do with when he was Greede's henchman and I kicked his ass a few times."

"No, he does not care about that," Greg said. "He told us he deserved everything he got back then. And that he does not want interaction with Greede now because he might kill him. But he dislikes you, Erik, because you are special to those important to him."

"But I have a girlfriend. Emphasis on *girl*."

"Love is irrational," Greg said sagely. "He is happy now, maybe for first time in his life. He only knows anger as means of protection. And there is also the way you look at yourself."

"What way?"

Greg raised his eyebrows. "You had bad few years. You died, you came back. You were demon, then you got magic. But through all that, you kept trying to be a better *person*. And all of us around you noticed. It is admirable. It is heroic, more heroic than picking up sword and slaying dragon."

"Actually, I rode a dragon once-"

"You have told story many times."

"And I intend to keep telling it until it stops being cool."

Greg scoffed and tossed me a protein bar. "Eat, then sleep. I will wake you up when sun come up."

I unwrapped that sucker and started eating with something like a vengeance. "How can you tell when the sun will be up? It's just rocks and ice down here. Will sunlight even reach this point?"

Greg gave me a sly look.

"I will know."

I WAS FLOATING. Very rarely do I have dreams where I just casually float around, so I tend to enjoy them on those rare occasions.

"Erik?"

I blinked something in my eyes and now I was in a room made entirely out of gold. Streaks of purple and blue energy ran through, illuminating furniture—bookshelves, tables, chairs—and as the energy passed through, the furniture went back to being invisible. It was like my eyes could not see that deeply. As if light simply would not reach my eyeballs.

But I could see her clearly.

She was five feet and change, slight of build, wearing her usual uniform of business slacks, riding boots, and an olive-green cape with a silver brooch clasp. Her hair was blonde to the point where it was white, and her eyes matched mine—green, oval, and curious.

Gil Ashendale stood up.

"What are you doing here?"

My sister ran forwards and was about to hug me, before retreating. "Are you astral-projecting? Because I can't touch you if you are astral-projecting. Wait, when did you learn how to astral-project?"

"Hey, sis," I said. "I have no idea what's going on."

She shook her head slightly.

"Where are you?" I asked. "Were you kidnapped?"

She raised her eyebrows. "Seriously?"

"Mephisto disappeared with you," I said.

"And you think someone can just take me *and* Mephisto without at least raising an alarm?" she demanded.

"Hey, don't get huffy with me, it looked suspicious to everyone," I snapped. "Now where the hell is this?"

"I don't know," she said. A smile stretched on her face. "It's a higher dimension from what I can tell. And Erik, I'm learning so much here. There's this Nexus in a dimension beneath the mansion and it's linked to those that came before us."

"Us?"

She nodded. "Not us, as in Ashendale. I mean us as a species. And angels, and demons, and their ancestors, too."

"Now, now!"

The new voice echoed from everywhere. It shook the whole world. Golden light flashed off all walls, blue and purple lightning zapped around, furniture appeared and disappeared, and finally a living supernova stood in front of me, right next to my sister.

It was hard to look at it, at least not until it took a vaguely human shape of a man wearing a long white robe with a sash of gold at the waist. His hair was long but it was his eyes that gave him away. He had two suns for eyes, massive white dwarfs rendered small enough to fit in his skull.

"Hello, Erik," Michael said.

Not awaiting my answer he looked at my sister and the

world shifted. She was no longer there.

"Where is she?" I demanded.

"Right where she was before you arrived," he said. "This place is rather handy like that. You should recognize it for it belongs to a higher power than myself."

It clicked as soon as he said it. I just had to picture a golden Chinese dragon floating in the air, and this was exactly where Sun Tzu had brought back my soul after I—with the help of my sister—had broken out of Limbo.

This was God's realm.

Or at the very least, God's country townhouse.

"Daddy lent you the keys to the apartment, huh?" I asked.

Michael smiled but said nothing.

"Heaven fell because you left."

He shook his head. "No. Everything is exactly as it should be. I will return soon, sooner than I intended." His expression darkened.

And no, I don't mean metaphorically. I mean, his face darkened and the room darkened along with it.

"Your actions are one such reason. Along with that whom you call Alan Greede. And his... sponsor."

I shuddered.

Michael took a deep breath and the darkness was no more.

"You seem keen on giving out answers to my sister," I said. "Any ideas on what that sponsor guy is?"

I knew enough by now not to mention Azazel by name.

Michael, who seemed to be reading my thoughts, nodded with approval. Oh goody—the guy with two suns in his eyes approves of my lack of stupidity.

Maybe there's hope for me yet.

"There is always hope," the angel said out loud, thus

confirming he *could* read my thoughts. "And no, I cannot tell. That creature escapes my comprehension. It is something more... or perhaps something *less*."

"Well, that's helpful."

"Your sibling seems to think so," Michael said. And there goes that typical angelic literalism. Even having a galaxy's worth of power in your system doesn't give you a sense of humor. Somethings you just gotta have, I suppose.

"Gil mentioned a Nexus-"

"That is enough," he said softly. Still, there was enough power in his words to knock the breath from my lungs. "She is to know, you are to do. That is who you are, Ashendale twins. Marked by destiny. You must fulfill your own paths before meeting. Now it is time for you to depart."

He raised his hand.

"I know not where you will end up in your world, since I have no familiarity with it. But please, make sure to find your way back to the Vault. It is important for all our sakes."

"Wait, what? Where are you sending me?"

"Allow me, please," came a new voice.

A man wearing a butler suit floated in, his expensive Italian loafers never once touching the ground. His ebony hair was tied back with a ribbon of midnight blue, and his eyes were an exact copy of Amaymon's.

Mephistopheles, elemental of air, brother of Amaymon, stood by Michael and nodded.

"Respectfully, I do know where to send him, and his species are not yet learned on how to traverse planets." He looked at me for the first time. "Hello, Master Erik."

"Mephisto, what the hell-"

"Goodbye, Master Erik."

He waved his hand and I was back to falling, falling, and more falling.

25

Once again, I woke up with a start. At least I managed not to scream this time. The dream, or vision, or whatever you want to call it, echoed vividly in my mind, conjuring more questions than answers.

Sunlight snuck in through the cave in a narrow beam, reflected off of the polished white surface of the ice that permeated every square inch of this land. I turned towards the makeshift door and discovered it had been opened.

Greg was nowhere to be seen.

Picking up Djinn and making sure I was well-dressed for outside weather, I crawled through the narrow space of the door, my shoulders scraping ice and frost as I went along. Finally, I found air and a lack of general resistance, and then I was out of the hole, and my face was immediately struck with a thousand little needles as the cold wind assaulted me.

Lying on the ground just a few feet away was a thick thermal jacket like the one we had been issued. There was little to no frost on it, which meant it wasn't one the golems had been wearing. A few feet further was Greg's shirt.

I looked up and saw a hill, maybe about five minutes climb if you watched your footing, two if you were a maverick and didn't much value your ankles. Sitting on top of the hill, shirtless and cross-legged in meditation, was Greg himself. As I approached (it took me about four minutes—I'm a maverick with some reservations) I noticed sunlight on his skin.

This wasn't the natural glow of skin beneath the sun either. This looked like that one scene from *Twilight* when the dumbass, emo vampire glows beneath the sun.

Sunlight seemed to be trapped beneath Greg's skin and rippling outwards, before sinking even deeper into his flesh. The result was a bizarre light show, as if someone had lit a thousand tiny flashlights beneath his skin and set their rhythm at random.

He had his eyes closed but when he opened them, they were electric blue and gold. He blinked a few times and rolled his shoulders.

"You are awake," he said without looking at me. "You were talking in your sleep. Was it productive at least?"

"Merely insightful," I replied, throwing his shirt and jacket a few inches from where he sat. "What are you doing?"

"Sunbathing," Greg replied.

I waited for a punchline that never came.

Greg chuckled. "You have question."

"I also have an observation," I said. "Like the fact my balls have retracted back into my lower intestines and I'm pretty sure most of my insides are icicles, and yet here you are 'sunbathing'. Is this a Kresnik thing?"

He stood up, calmly brushing snow off his person, and picked up the shirt.

"Yes," he said. "It is one of my abilities. Just as vampires gain strength at night, I as their opposite, gain strength from daylight and sun." He frowned. "Well, also moonlight. Is practically same thing."

Taking up the jacket, he put it on, zipped up, and tapped something metallic buried in the snow. With a flick of his boot, his cruciform spear flew into the air. He caught it and twirled it once to shake the snow off it.

"Come. We must get guns and move on," he said, making his way down the hill. "I have located path for us to follow."

Back at the cave, we managed to pull out a functional rifle each and as much sleeping gear as we could carry. Greg had a single blanket bundled up on a light backpack that was mostly filled with food.

"So you can absorb sunlight," I said, as we marched towards the valley, "and you can locate vampires."

"Yes," he replied.

"And you don't absorb blood."

"Of course not."

"Just sunlight." I chuckled. "Like a plant. Like an undead-slaying plant."

Greg paused, turned to give me an annoyed look and shook his head. "I am not plant. Plant has leaves."

"I'll get you some leaves," I went on. "Make 'em into a hula skirt."

"I was in Hawaii once," he said. "Very nice place."

"They have vampires in Hawaii? Isn't that place just, like, constant sunlight, seawater, and fat tourists?"

Greg chuckled. "Yes. But this was not for vampire."

"Then what?"

"Evil guardian spirit," he said, shuddering. "Very powerful magic. Very bad for locals."

"How does a guardian spirit go ba-"

The rude Yeti never let me finish my sentence.

It emerged out of nowhere, slammed an ape-like fist into my side, and I was sent flying. Greg's rifle went off, and blood flew from a second Yeti that was encroaching on him. The rifle coughed bullets for a while and then choked up. Swearing in Russian, Greg took the weapon off and launched it towards another Yeti, his spear flashing after it. The blade pierced the beast and sent it screaming away from him.

I shook the stars from my head and sat up. A Yeti was looming over me. I let out a blast of concussive magical force that threw the beast away from me.

More of them popped up, their white hides making it impossible to properly discern how many there were in contrast to the snow.

"Run!" I wasn't sure if Greg or I said it first, or if we both had the same idea at the same time, but I knew we took off like crazy, tearing through the valley while a horde of Yetis chased after us.

The snow made us slower and they were quickly gaining on us.

Something clicked in my head.

"Magic," I said. "They can manipulate the snow."

Greg's response was to throw a vial of a grey liquid that, upon exploding, filled the area with thick black smoke. He dodged to one side as a Yeti barely passed him, his spear slicing a neat gash along its side. A second one narrowly avoided taking his head off.

I wasn't so graceful. I'm more of a tank, so when the first Yeti reached me, shadows grew from my body and latched onto it. The Yeti and shadows started a tug of war, which I ended with a quick thrust from Djinn. My pistol roared in my left hand, crippling and maiming anyone it hit.

But there were more of them. Many many more.

Suddenly, a massive trumpet-like sound.

For a brief moment I thought it was the angels coming to rescue us. The sound resembled exaltation in video games —you know, when the cavalry arrives to save the heroes from being totally massacred.

But there were no angels.

They looked like buildings, swaying from side to side, until they came into view. Quadrupeds with a hunched back, long, muscle-laced legs that ended in curved claws perfect for climbing, shattering ice, or tearing flesh off of unfortunate Wizards. Thick manes of white fur drooped from their bodies, the longer strands actually scraping along the icy floor. Their elephantine features consisted of mammoth tusks that curved outwards and branched out into multiple spikes. Trunks ended in a pair of blades that were duller than I remembered — or perhaps this was a different sub-species.

"Behemoths," I heard myself say.

I had fought Behemoths before.

Correction, *a* Behemoth.

A Behemoth that was too small to fully manifest and that had taken over an elephant in a zoo. The same Behemoth whose ectoplasm Amaymon had infused to the gun I had used for years, the same one Jack had remodeled into the version currently in my hands.

These were the snowier version of that one and clearly, they were adult-sized. And there was at least a dozen of them.

The Yetis all screamed and ran away—smart Yetis— while Greg and I remained rooted on the spot, putting a big caveat into the whole people-are-smarter-than-apes argument.

The first Behemoth lurched forward and leaned down. His trunk—big enough to wrap around a couple of cars and turn them into pencils—swished close to me. I blocked those stubby blades with my shortsword and fought back. Shadows billowed from me as I called my magic.

The Behemoth retreated and raised its trunk in the air.

"Uh oh," I muttered.

Greg lowered his stance, spear ready. "Erik, what did I tell you about piss off big creatures?"

"Make sure to have a really big sword if you do?"

The Behemoth let out another bellow and his trunk lowered. It went straight for my left hand.

My gun.

"You want this?" I thrust the weapon forwards and charged it with magic.

The big monster lowered its head to inspect it, unaware or uncaring of the blasting magic I was about unleash on its face. Its trunk poked the gun, tapping it gently with the blades and then it looked at me.

Eyes the size of tractor tires blinked and the massive beast sank on its forelegs, like a camel, then its hind legs.

And there it sat, watching me.

I lowered the gun. "Um..."

"Erik," Greg said. "You have Behemoth in gun. That beast once recognized you as master. Maybe this one does, too."

I looked from the gun to the beast. The rest of the pack, all two dozen of them, also sat down, gently as you please, on the freezing snow.

"Um... Hi," I said.

The Behemoth kept staring at me.

Taking a deep breath, I reached out. The Behemoth arced its trunk and I felt its thick hide beneath. Aware of those blades on either side of my body, I was very careful to pat it as nicely as I could.

The beast did not pull back.

Instead it made a rumbling noise.

One of the Behemoths at the back made a trumpeting noise and now all of them were agitated. Climbing back to his feet, the big one in front of me wrapped his trunk around my waist and before I knew what was happening, it had hoisted me over its back.

Another one had done the same to Greg.

They turned. From this height I could now see what had caught their attention.

On the other side of the valley were a series of flashing lights.

Angels!

Gabriel's forces had found us.

"There," I said. "Take us there."

The Behemoth I was riding made a trumpeting noise again, and he took off with me holding onto its fur for dear life.

26

One of the most thrilling moments in my career was getting to ride a dragon as it chased a helicopter.

Riding a Behemoth had to be a close second.

Every step crossed huge distances, and the wind up there was twice as strong. Luckily, I had a giant demon head to shield my delicate one from shards of ice. The landscape below us skated by as if I was on a plane. Surprisingly, the jarring was minimal. Not only was the thick fur great at shock absorption, but the Behemoth's long legs and tipped claws had great stability, those flat, wide, echinoderm paws latching onto the ground, claws securing against any slipping. The Behemoths also had narrow bodies when compared to their remarkable heights. I would even say their shoulders were narrow in comparison to the other Behemoth I had seen at the zoo some eight years ago.

Hurray for smart evolution.

The lights of battle came ever closer and as we climbed over the valley's crest, the scene was pretty clear. Our side had been reduced down to just the core members.

The Grigori (sans Greg who had latched on his Behemoth with a permanent frown and a stiff posture), along with Greede, six rogue angels led by Anael, and the two Fey, Niamh and Morgana, were battling a metric fuckton of angels.

Gabriel himself was locked in a dogfight with Anael in the air, bolts of energy lancing from his sword.

Beyond them, the landscape was shimmering. At first I thought it was just the heat haze from the fight, but upon further inspection I recognized the tell-tale signs of a really, really good illusion spell. I would have never recognized it were it not for the years I had spent with Abi and her amazing talents, and the fact that I was so high up, I could see a tiny bit of the circumference of the spell.

Unless you knew the parameters of the spell, such as the building or person you were trying to hide, you weren't supposed to see the edges—unless you had a bird's-eye view and knew what to look for.

This spell was powerful. Too powerful to be cast by just one person, which led me to think that it was both old and a team effort.

"The Vault," I said. Then, yelling, so Greg can hear, "Greg, see that shimmer?"

"No," he said. "I only see battle."

"It's there, trust me," I said. "It's the Vault."

"Then we must act," Greg said. "How do I lower this beast? I must go help my allies."

"No need, little Kresnik."

The voice was accompanied by a thunder. A flash of lightning exploded before us, and Perun, all eight feet of him, rolled his shoulders. A weapon that looked like a cross between a great axe and a maul, was across his back.

Perun stroked his lightning-charged beard and looked at the Behemoths.

And the fucking Behemoths trembled.

Like goddamn puppies.

"*Bozhe moi*," he said. "You ride demons, little wizard. Is good. Shows potential. Now send them away."

As if reading his mind, the Behemoths reached with their trunks and deposited me and Greg on the ground. Then they turned tail and ran.

Actually *ran*.

I glanced at the running demons, then at the god, then at the scene behind him.

"Let me guess," I said, "we're in the right place."

Perun chuckled. "You are funny. I like that. Funny people scream loudest when they die." He turned his storm-filled eyes towards Greg and said something in Russian.

Greg lowered his spear and then bowed.

Perun laughed in his face.

"I am not your god, Kresnik. Bowing is for sycophants and pussies. You are neither."

"I was showing respect to an old god," Greg replied.

"Bah! Respect is shown through action and bloodshed," Perun said. "Now come. Gold One is about to spank children behaving badly."

He led us towards the battlefield, where I noticed that several of the other gods had appeared.

Hela, Ganesh, Zeus, Kagu-Tsuchi, and Cernunnos simply manifested, their collective presence enough to quell the battle.

Not Gabriel though. He kept on going.

Until Sun Tzu bitch-slapped him into the ground and glided next to him.

"Cease your bickering," he snapped.

Sun Tzu never snaps. But here's the thing about gods: when they get pissed off, you listen.

Gabriel rubbed his cheek and his hand came back with golden ichor.

"The time for this battle is over," Sun Tzu announced. He then saw us coming. "Ah, Perun. Erik. Greg. Thank you for joining us. You should not have been separated."

"We had to be heroic," I said.

"There are many dangers guarding the Vault," Hela hissed.

I tried to grin at her, while forcing myself not to throw up when looking at her zombie side.

"We took care of them."

"We ran for long time," Greg said. "And hid in cave."

I rolled my eyes at him. "Yeah, leave out the part where we rode actual Behemoths. Like that's not cool or anything."

"It was very cool. So cool it was freezing," Greg said, with a grin.

"Dude, no. Leave the jokes to the professionals."

"If you are quite done," Zeus thundered. "We have to get this over with. I cannot stay long."

Sun Tzu nodded at him and I wondered what could be more important than saving the world from a demon, but hey — that's a god for you.

"There will be a cease-fire amongst all of you," Sun Tzu announced.

Perun's axe thunked hard on the ice and sent a menacing vibration. He didn't have to say "or else."

Anael nodded at Sun Tzu. Emrys, too. When Sun Tzu looked at me, I gave a nod as well. Greede shrugged and raised his right wrist, where I saw a power-dampening bracelet.

Then the avatar looked at Gabriel whose eyes were

darting from god to god. I knew he was calculating the odds of taking them all down. I also knew which conclusion he would reach before he was nodding his submission.

"Excellent," Sun Tzu said. And just like that, he spun on his heels and walked straight into the illusion's haze.

27

Seven gods, two fairies, six humans, one slime, seven good angels, and way more evil ones, all walk into a bar...

Except the bar is a thousand-year-old prison, there's a demon inside, and three of us have magical nukes that serve as keys.

Ever feel like life is just one bad joke?

I expected the entrance to be a sigil-covered floor, maybe with a few guardians, magic of some sort, but instead we walked into an empty foyer.

Empty, grey, and completely lifeless.

The others must have felt it, too. Suddenly we were no longer tense and ready to fight. I saw angel shoulders slump, their wings drooping as if wanting nothing more than to fall asleep. The only one unaffected was Gabriel, which confirmed that what I was feeling was the effect of the Sin of Sloth.

The gods looked around curiously, probably seeing something invisible to the rest of us, and some—mostly

Ganesh—were murmuring amongst themselves. I was too busy trying to keep my eyes open.

Never before had a Sin affected me this much just by sheer proximity. That spoke volumes not just to its power, but more importantly to the host demon's strength as well. Belphegor was nothing to scoff at. If he had been even a fraction more awake, then this battle would have been over before we made it through the door—this was the level of enemy we were dealing with.

Suddenly I no longer wanted to fight. I wanted to forget about this whole thing and go back home. Go find Abi and spend a long day in bed, being lazy and happy. Hell, we wouldn't even need to talk—just enjoy *being* together. All I had to do was just walk away and...

NO!

I shook my head. No, this was the Sin's effect on me. I looked up and saw Greede grinning knowingly at me. I flipped him the bird. He scowled.

Point, Erik.

Footsteps echoed from the distance. Shadows seemed to angle away, as if the sun had decided to pass by. As the shadows moved, I saw a single door ahead of us. This door had no handle, no hinges, no means of opening or closing, but the footsteps were coming from it, and before I could register how or why, a man walked through the door and out towards us.

The first thing I noticed were his eyes. I have seen all kinds before: demonic, angelic, broken, happy, healthy. Eyes of people with hope, even if they don't show it; eyes of innocents looking in wonder at the world; eyes of those who were chewed up and spat back out by the world.

This man had all of those. Eyes of hope and misery. Eyes

of death and life. Eyes that warned us to leave, yet pleaded with us to stay.

They were brown and gold, marking him as an angel. He wore armor that desperately needed a polish and was perhaps two sizes too big for him. Some of it had rusted off and been discarded, revealing a thin wiry figure beneath that looked gaunt enough to be sick and malnourished.

His wings were minuscule, folded behind him. They were grey and withered, and for a second I believed him to be Fallen, before realizing I had seen these symptoms before: the exact same thing was happening to Jehudiel. This guy was being starved from his connection to Heaven and was on his last legs. He carried no weapons whatsoever, and he was out of breath by the time he made it before us.

"Welcome," he said. His voice had a wheezing rasp to it as if it hadn't been used in quite some time. "You seek the Vault. You have found it."

Sun Tzu stepped forwards, along with Gabriel, Anael, and Emrys. The four leaders of four different factions that had led to this epic clusterfuck.

Sun Tzu bowed deeply. "Master Guardian, archangel Uriel, Virtue of Generosity. I thank thee."

Uriel swept a long strand of black greasy hair from his face, threw his head back and laughed. Now I could see the archangel part. His laugh was like a singing choir.

"It has been so many years, so many decades, since I heard my own name uttered," he said.

He approached Sun Tzu and gave the old man a hug.

Gabriel and Anael were immediately on their knees. Now, you have to understand that those two were also archangels, and Virtues, and they just bowed in reverence to this guy that looked like a stage-four cancer patient.

Uriel patted each on their heads before saying, "Rise, children. My, how you have grown."

From their blushing you would have thought the two angels kids getting a compliment for the first time in their lives.

He nodded at Emrys. "Master Druid. You have kept your promise. You and your... sponsor."

The angel's eyes travelled to the gods and settled on Cernunnos, who inclined his horned head ever so slightly.

Then Uriel backed away a little and announced in a voice that rang with power:

"For five hundred years I have watched over my charge," he began.

My jaw dropped.

Five hundred years?

Jehudiel was in trouble after just one. This guy had been cut off from Heaven for five hundred freaking years? No wonder everyone was treating him like royalty. At full power, this guy could rival Michael himself.

"Now it is time," he went on. "The Vault shall be opened again. Have you the keys?"

Sun Tzu nodded and backed away. Zeus broke rank and thrust his chest out proudly as he walked towards Uriel. A shield of brass manifested in his hands and he passed it reverently to Uriel. Perun rolled his eyes behind him and made gagging noises while winking at me.

"I want that back," Zeus told the angel.

"Of course," Uriel said, taking the shield. Even if it was taller than he was by a full foot, he lifted it easily and pressed it against the door he had appeared from. The metal rippled and for a second I imagined myself back in Michael's room, inside that pool of energy.

The shield sank into the door and hung suspended in the middle.

Emrys looked at Cernunnos. The god gave a nod. Emrys took out a leaf from his pocket and whispered something to it. The Spear of the Sun emerged in a nightly glow of light, blinding us for a moment. The Druid handed the weapon over and Uriel thrust it into the door. It was also absorbed and came to rest across the Aegis shield.

Seneschal thrust Greede forward and released him, unwrapping a gooey tendril from the man's left hand, while simultaneously working a key to unlock the power-dampening bracelet. I tensed for a minute as Greede rubbed his wrists with a sigh of relief. He summoned the Necronomicon. It was smoking. Greede quickly found the page where the Sword of Michael was—the page where all the smoke was coming from—and tore it out.

The gargantuan sword manifested. Uriel gracefully took to the air and caught it by the handle before it could fall on Greede, then hoisted the weapon into the door. It sunk in and came to rest across the Aegis shield as well but on the other side.

Greede backed away hurriedly from Uriel.

"The keys are in place," Uriel said. "Now only one of you may pass through the door. One whom I will deem worthy. Please, bring forth your champions."

Uriel spread his arms. Spheres of light billowed out of his body and swirled around our entire group. Emrys looked down as some of them became attached to him. Gabriel, too, was chosen.

"Erik," I heard Greg saying.

I looked down. My black coat shone like someone had draped fairy lights over me. I stepped forwards.

Behind me I heard footsteps and Greede joined me.

"Him?" I blurted out.

"Worthiness comes in many shades, mortal," Uriel reprimanded me. "The Druid has belief. Gabriel has loyalty. You have courage. Alan Greede has determination."

"Gotta have that to be a villain," I said.

"Don't assume anything, Mr. Ashendale," Greede said with a grin. "I am merely determined to make the world a better place."

"Silence!" Uriel said. "Four are chosen, one must pass."

As he spoke I felt his words perforate into my mind. It was like there was a mini-angel inside my brain, pressing against my defenses, probing at me. I didn't like that.

I could feel that something was off here. It was as if I could sense a threat, a connection, but couldn't *see* it. Something connected Uriel to the gods, to Greede, to Gabriel, to Gil, to me... it was all one big strategy, one play of a master chess player.

I opened my eyes just as Uriel stopped before Greede. My blood chilled as he placed his hand on the latter's shoulder.

"Alan Greede, you are worthy to enter the Vault. Belphegor and the Sin of Sloth are yours."

28

It was one of those rare occasions where everyone, friend and foe, protested the same idea.

All of us in the room turned to look at Greede, weapons gripped, scowls painted on, and me yelling,

"Are you fucking kidding me? *Him?* You have gods and literal fucking angels and you went with the psychopath bent on world domination?"

Uriel remained unfazed.

"So it is chosen," he said. "So mote it be."

The door behind him split at an invisible seam and opened a crack, just enough for a man of Greede's stature to pass through. He took his first steps forwards. I drew out my sword, and lunged at him, just as Seneschal stepped in and lunged at Greede at the same time. The slime's arm collided with my side and I was sent skidding to the side.

Gabriel threw himself at Greede next, along with Emrys, Anael, two of the closest rogue angels and Greg. Uriel swept his right hand casually. A blast of invisible force threw them all backwards.

Greede grinned at us. He spun on his heels and began briskly walking towards the open Vault door.

"Help us," I cried to the gods.

But they all stood there, still as statues, even Perun whom I could tell was itching to swing his axe at Greede. Sun Tzu shot him a warning look and then turned a frigid gaze towards me.

It's incredible how one moment, one single look, can shatter a lifetime of amicability. I'd always had a good relationship with Sun Tzu. I saw him as a father figure. But I had made one incalculable error: I had seen him as human.

He was not.

The Grigori threw themselves against Uriel, while Gabriel's angels tried to get Greede. Uriel altered a fire blast from Luke and halted their advance, before appearing before them and blasting them away. Mustafa set about chanting, and I felt the beginnings of an Abjuration spell, one that was meant to siphon off some of the archangel's energy.

I called upon my shadows and felt my body change. Every muscle was on fire. Djinn glowed azure as I swung it towards Uriel. Anael joined me, along with Gabriel, and we struck together. Uriel stumbled backwards, just enough for Morgana and Niamh to double-team him with sword and spear, leaving Emrys to turn into a bear and barrel straight into him.

"Erik." Evans the golem come up behind me. "You must catch Greede. Stop him now."

"He's too far."

"No, he is not." The golem grinned.

Then he grabbed the scruff of my coat, wound up his arm, and threw me across the room.

"GREEDE!"

He turned. The Necronomicon was in his hands. My sword met the book, ripped it, and both of us went flying through the door.

Greede cried out as he clutched his side. My sword had grazed more than just the book it seemed. I climbed to my feet.

The room was circular and glowing white and blue. Heavenly colors, I realized. Light came from a series of geometrical grooves that were etched into the walls. In the middle of the room was a...

Thing.

It looked like a giant, but parts of it had melted. It was as if someone had tried to create a man from scratch with only rudimentary knowledge of where things need to go, and abandoned the project halfway, leaving it into the middle of a furnace to melt.

Belphegor was not a pretty boy.

Half his face was melted into pinkish-grey wax, while the other half was all eyes and teeth, some poking into one another. It had multiple hands—not arms, mind you, just the hands—poking out of its torso, and several tendril-like appendages with claws and fingers on them. His legs were a cross between hooves and feet, the feet turned backwards.

It had wings too, and a mane of back hair that looked like someone had tried to make a cape out of shag carpeting.

In the middle of its chest was a single eye, and that eye was pierced with the largest metal stake I had ever seen in my life. Seriously, there were concrete support bars smaller than this thing. The stake pinned the beast to the ground, while a series of silver-grey chains were tied, nailed, and otherwise attached to the primordial demon.

And *still,* it yawned and pried open its giant eye, along with a few that were scattered over its hide.

The demon shifted and then went back to sleep. If its bonds were hurting it, it didn't show. Only the slight shifting of its tentacles and twitching of eyes indicated it was actually alive.

That, and the mass of power coming from it. I can't describe the level of power. It was beyond the ocean and the sky. It was something utterly abhorrent.

This was worse than death. This was sloth to the point of expiration.

Literal nonexistence.

"It's not a demon," I said.

Greede opened the Necronomicon and chuckled. "Took you long enough to figure it out."

Our attacks met in the middle. A blast of purple energy from him, and a blue one from me. I rolled, came up with my gun and blasted off. A shadow tendril whipped at him. Greede conjured a barrier and slipped past it, letting my tendril crush the spell without harming him. Bullets whizzed past him as the Necronomicon opened.

A bulbous ape-like arm emerged from the book just as Greede dropped it.

A second arm came out, followed by a swollen, wide-eyed head with horns, a bloated body with smaller arms poking out of its sides, and a pair of stubby legs that could barely support the demon's weight.

"Mammon," I said. "That's the Sin of Greed."

It had never come out of the book before, usually emerging from within Greede himself.

"I knew you were bullshitting," I told Greede. "The power was too good."

"Oh, my dear Erik Ashendale," he said. "You have no idea what I am capable of." He slapped the demon on the arm. "Distract him."

Mammon splayed its arms. Golden sigils formed in the air. I grabbed Djinn with both hands, channeling power into the weapon so that the blade elongated. While Mammon charged his spell, my sword swelled ten times its normal size and I swung. The energy sword cut through glowing stone and one of Belphegor's chains, and slammed into Mammon. His spell shattered before it could be completed, and the backlash of all that energy aided my attack.

Mammon was sent flying to the side, broken and bloodied. Greede clicked his tongue in annoyance.

"He's been annoyed with me ever since I cast him out," he said conversationally. "I wasn't lying about that. That Sin was Azazel's gift, and that guy is about as anal as they come. So I removed Mammon before he could take it, and stored the power inside the Necronomicon."

"How is that even possible?" I asked.

"I'm a really smart cookie," he replied. "And you have been asking the wrong questions. All of you."

I raised my sword. "Oh yeah?"

"Yes, indeed," he said. "You see, you assumed I gave up the mantle of power. Why would I do such a thing? There's an old adage: never let go of something unless you have a replacement."

I looked at the slumbering demon behind him. "You want that one instead?"

"I'm a greedy boy," he said. "I want them all."

"You can barely handle one, Greede," I said. "And this bullshit is over."

I lunged at him. He didn't dodge. Maybe I was too fast but I knew something was wrong. It was too late now. I charged up magic, ready to tank whatever trap he set up...

And a maw opened in front of me.

One moment there was Greede, the next a vertical

mouth split open the fabric of reality, eight feet of teeth, ectoplasmic saliva, and a deep abyss beyond.

I screamed and threw myself aside. My shadows latched onto the ground. An instant later they were sucked in by the maw, and suddenly I was back to normal, all my magic sucked away.

I swung a normal-sized Djinn at the maw, catching one of the teeth. As soon as I made contact, I felt my life force being drained away. Magic pumped into my body, but the more I used the more I fed this thing.

Once I was on my knees, my body shaking, and feeling like I had been starved for a decade, the maw shrunk. Greede reappeared, the maw disappearing into his stomach. He was shirtless now, with his jacket in shreds draped around his shoulders.

"Thank you for that test," he said, removing the shreds. "I was wondering if this new Sin was powerful enough to withstand your remarkable magical volume. It seems I was right."

"What… is that?" I panted.

"This is the Sin of Gluttony," Greede said. "I came across it very early on and it took me decades to figure out how to separate it from Beelzebub, the original host. In fact, the only way I managed was to kill him before the two could fully merge. And after the disastrous affair with Azazel and the Knightmare… Let's just say I was more than incentivized to upgrade."

He reached out and patted the sleeping Belphegor on the arm.

"And Belphegor here was all part of the plan from the start. You see, this was the one Sin that Azazel could not get to thanks to the Grigori. But I could. All I had to do was play my cards right. Only you thought it was a demon—this is no demon. Not even a proto-demon. This is an Outsider, a being of pure chaos that got trapped into a physical form long ago when the universe was still trying to figure itself out. It lay dormant because that is the only thing it *can* do whilst in our universe. Indirect interaction and all that. Until Azazel released the Sins and Belphegor here found himself with a cell mate."

"Just like Azazel," I said. "He's an Outsider too."

Greede chuckled.

"Oh, I lied about that," he said. "Belphegor is the Outsider, not Azazel. I confess I have no idea what that guy is—except that whatever he is, he is weakened. Hence his need for the Sins."

I managed to stand back up, using my sword to help lever myself. As soon as I did, Mammon's massive fist punched into me and I slammed into a wall and slumped back down.

"Pathetic," Greede said. "Come, Mammon. Join us."

The demon lumbered towards its former host, Greede's stomach split, teeth on either side, and the maw absorbed Mammon.

Instantly, Greede grew by a few feet, his body swelling out. The maw's teeth jutted out like thorns, and he turned towards Belphegor.

"Belphegor yearns release," he said. "Once I take the Sin, it will be free."

"You'll kill us all," I rasped. "You can't control an Outsider."

Greede spread his arms towards Belphegor. The chains snapped, leaving only the giant stake. It vibrated so rapidly the edges were smudged. A crack appeared along it with the sound of a gunshot.

Belphegor was free. The beast opened his eyes and

stared at Greede. It moaned and then choked on something wet and gelatinous. Greede giggled as he latched onto the Outsider and his stomach teeth pierced into the awakened beast.

"Now, Gluttony. Consume!"

I could feel Sloth struggling against Greede, but the latter had two Sins versus its one. I began shaking and feeling sick. This was chaos being released. Anti-life.

I had to stop this.

I just hoped this place got good reception.

Greede turned his head towards me when he saw me chuckle. "What is so amusing?"

"You," I said, pulling out a receiver from my coat pocket. "And your big fat mouth. You always liked the sound of your own voice, Greede, and no matter how much power you obtain, you will always be that asshole who talks too much. And that's your downfall."

Before he could react I pressed the button, opened the channel and screamed,

"Abi, now! Do it now!"

29

"Are you sure?" Abi looked up from the notes, a dark frown etched on her features. "Erik, this is not good. I mean look at it... this is designed against *you*."

I scanned over the blueprints of Project Icarus.

"Gil designed it to take down the Knightmare," I said. "It's meant to counter a demonic invasion, just like the one I brought on Greede's stronghold."

Abi nodded. "It is. And I can see why she did it. I mean, I knew she was working on something big, but this..."

"What does it do, exactly?" I asked. "I can see the satellites here, but what sort of damage are we looking at?"

"Ashendale satellites here, here, and here," she said pointing at blank spaces on the map. "Armed with ballistic missiles and a compound of magical anti-material. It's a variation of the process to create wands."

"Having a real Druid around really helped," I said.

"Actually it was Greede's company," Abi said. "Greede and Ryleh Corp had multiple magical weapons. Gil repurposed them and launched them in space."

She fiddled with the console and pulled up a damage simulation.

"It's about sixteen hundred megatons."

"That's a lot of megatons," I commented.

"All dispersing anti-magic and anti-material," Abi said. "Erik, if we use this, nothing will survive. Antarctica will not be the same."

"And if Greede takes power, or Sloth is released, or the angels invade, the world won't be the same," I countered. "What's the range of this thing?"

"No limit."

"So I can pinpoint a location and... ka-boom?"

"Yes."

I took a deep breath. "Okay. Okay."

She snaked her hand on mine. "What are you thinking?"

"I'm thinking I wanna go on vacation," I told her. "Somewhere warm. With sand and palm trees."

"You hate the beach," she said.

"But you don't."

She squeezed my hand. We stayed like that for a moment.

Then I had to ruin it. "Set it online," I said. "And be ready for my signal."

"Abi, now! Do it now!"

Want to know what sixteen megatons of ka-boom sounds like?

Me too.

But you never hear stuff like that. The missiles hit before

sound could register. The world went really bright, and then there was fire, and then there was nothing.

AND THEN PAIN.

Pain radiated throughout my body and man was I relieved. Pain was great. Pain meant I was alive.

The events of what I had just done transpired in my head again and I tried sitting up, only I was missing a good portion of my lower body.

How was I still alive?

Shadows billowed from me like a fine dark mist, becoming more solid as I removed myself from beneath rubble. Crawling was much easier without them pesky legs.

I felt my magic kick into overdrive.

The sensations were bizarre and completely alien, and since I imagine none of you ever regrew a limb, then you can't possibly know what it would be like.

My right arm clicked and popped, and suddenly it had full range of motion. My left was okay, and wouldn't you know, I found my weapons lying about not too far away.

Djinn was intact but my gun was a pancake. I managed to get it into my coat, which thanks to its enchantments had managed to survive, and that's when my legs grew back. Enough of my clothes had survived to keep me decent.

It's the little things in life.

Wait, that didn't come out right.

I stood up and surveyed the damage.

The Vault had taken most of the impact and dispersed it —which made me wonder what kind of power it had taken to erect such a barrier, and how freaking strong it would have been had it not stood here in the cold eroding for a couple of centuries.

Also, there was no Vault now. It was just a plain, sort-of-flat, landscape. Around us were a dozen craters, but like I said, the magic on the Vault had saved us from caving in.

It had also saved my friends.

One by one the Grigori made it out. Mustafa, to his credit, had conjured a protective shield quickly and saved a few lives. Most of the angels, save Gabriel, Anael, and two more, had been atomized. (No worries, they were just going to reappear in Heaven where they belonged.)

Niamh and Morgana had leapt on Emrys and shielded him with their own brand of magic, but both of them looked like they were on their last legs. Emrys himself was staring around, tears in his eyes, as he saw the magnitude of damage I had wrought on the South Pole.

"What did you do?" he asked, horror in his voice.

"What I had to," I said. "Greede tricked us. He has another Sin, Gluttony, and he can absorb others with it. He's already taken Greed. I stopped him from taking Sloth."

"Oh, did you now?"

Rubble exploded from a few feet away, and out came Alan Greede, swollen with muscle. Horns jutted out of his head, along with a mass of tentacles from his back. His aura was so powerful it was affecting physical matter around him. Bits of debris floated around him and were flung upwards, caught in the sheer vortex that was his existence.

I swore and grasped my sword tighter.

"You cannot beat me, Erik Ashendale," he said. "I have three Sins. I am powerful."

Then he threw his head upwards and roared,

"Do you hear me? I have *three*. So go on then! Send him! Send the Calamity to stop me if you dare!"

"What are you doing?" Anael yelled. Her spear trembled in her hands. "The Calamity! You cannot be serious."

He grinned at her.

"He speaks the truth."

I turned to see all the gods that had been present before reappear. It satisfied me to see some of them bleeding. Well done, Gil. That's one big bomb.

"The Calamity will soon arrive," said Sun Tzu.

"Then stop him!" I cried.

He shook his head. "It is not our place yet."

"Bullshit!"

"Now, now, Mr. Ashendale," Greede taunted. "Is that any way to speak to your elders?" He lowered himself into a deep bow at the waist. "Thank you, oh gods. Things worked out splendidly."

I looked from the gods to Greede and then all fell in place.

"You were working with him," I said. "This was all a set up. You set up Greede to obtain Sloth." No response from them. "But why?"

"Balance," Ganesh said. "His power will trigger another, which in turn will trigger a third, and the balance will be achieved."

"Power on one side will reveal power on the other," Zeus added. "We must expose the true danger if we are to defeat it."

Greede threw his head back and laughed. It sounded like a thousand glasses being shattered and scraped.

"You can never beat Azazel," he said. "You don't even know what it is. But I can. I have come the closest to it in power. Three Sins out of seven. Soon to be four."

He turned his gaze towards the rest of us.

"But it seems I have some time to kill. And speaking of killing-"

He launched himself at Emrys. The fey intercepted him.

Greede knocked them aside with a flick of his wrist. Emrys summoned his own magic and a green beam of power shot at Greede. The latter stumbled backwards.

"Horned One," he called. Cernunnos inclined his head. "My task is complete, aye?"

"Aye," the god replied. "Thou art free to act upon thy will alone."

Emrys shot Greede a predatory look. "Fucking A. Grigori, form up. Erik, frontal attack!"

"Fucking A," I replied.

And I threw myself at Greede who blocked with an invisible barrier. Undeterred, I threw a fireball at him, which he deflected. It was caught by Luke who turned it into an inferno. Greede transmuted the fire into air, which he sent towards Anael who was thrown off-course. Gabriel swung his sword, but Greede was no longer there, and the sword came down on Mustafa...

Who displaced himself by a few inches and looked like he was about to vomit.

"CEASE!"

Uriel erupted into view in a flash of light and pointed menacingly at Greede.

"Call not upon the Calamity," he yelled. "Renounce your proclamation, sorcerer. Do it now."

Greede cocked his head. "No, I don't think so."

"Then death it is."

Uriel took a single step forward.

SCHLICK!

The wet, sickening crunch of blood and bone was accompanied by the last few inches of Gabriel's long sword emerging out of Uriel's front.

"NO!"

Anael leapt...

Seneschal was on her, a blob of spikes and blades, and he shredded her wings until she was bloody and screaming.

"What are you-"

Emrys' scream was cut off as Seneschal appeared next to him. His arm was a blade, and he drew it across the Druid's throat. Blood sputtered and shot. The Fey screamed as their charge fell, gurgling blood.

Seneschal lunged, his amorphous form elongating to a point and found Mustafa's side. He gored him and passed through, punching into Greg with so much force he sent him into Evans. The golem was heavily damaged and the two fell over.

Seneschal stood still for the first time. Gabriel shot a beam of light at Luke that sent him spinning in the air and down to the ground and came to stand next to Seneschal.

And their faces matched.

Seneschal touched Gabriel's shoulder and the archangel melted, becoming amorphous and drawn into Seneschal's body until the latter stood by himself.

All the while Greede was in hysterics.

"This is too easy," he said. "I mean, honestly did you think I would not have someone to watch my back?"

I ran over to Emrys. Already he was applying earth-healing magic to his wound. The blood loss was stemmed but the guy wasn't going anywhere.

"I mean," Greede went on, "I even told you to your face I recognized the Slime as the creation of a former ally, and you still put him as my guardian. And the Druid! I knew you were locked thanks to your god's orders. And you, Mr. Ashendale."

His aura flared in my direction. I stood there and took it, but I was starting to feel the aftereffects of my heavy magic use. My tank was huge but reconstructing a human body in seconds took quite the surplus.

"You are the unfortunate scab in my plans," he said. "But it all worked out. I mean, I knew Michael was going to disappear three years ago. It was the perfect opportunity for some resurrection—do you remember that, Mr. Ashendale? Your death was no accident. That *thing* that killed you doesn't come out unless it's an apocalyptic event. I had no idea at the time but you were a key ingredient to resurrecting Belial, the Demon Emperor.

"Oh, I didn't care what happened afterwards, you see. The resurrection caused Michael to stay longer where the Calamity could track him and set its sights on him properly.

"Then came the second part of my plan. I had to destabilize both Heaven and Hell, you see, both neighbors of our earthly plane so that the ripples would merge and resonate. Breaking Heaven was obscenely easy. Corrupt one cog, abduct him six months before and replace him with a doppelgänger—I already had the synth-angel formula prepared and Bionoids already made the perfect duplicates. But to be sure, I told *my* Gabriel to go to war. All I had to do was give him an enemy to focus on: You."

Greede walked towards Uriel's body and unceremoniously lifted him off the ground.

"I have already taken Gabriel's grace and Virtue," he said. "He was the counter to Sloth, you see. Pre-planning, Mr. Ashendale. It's all about having a plan. I would have never been able to take Sloth had I not destroyed his Grace already. And this one-"

He shook Uriel's lifeless body, before plunging a fist inside his chest. I knew what he was doing—I had seen it before. Greede tore out Uriel's heart. Gluttony's maw opened in his chest and he tossed it in.

Power exploded from him.

"Uriel is Gluttony's counter," Greede said. "Michael placed him in the Vault because he knew Gluttony was the most dangerous Sin in the right hands. No offensive power to speak of but like I said, Mr. Ashendale, if you have a plan…"

Uriel's corpse began turning to ash. Greede tossed it aside.

"Bring me Gabriel," he told Seneschal. "I want him to witness this and kill him finally."

Seneschal nodded. He pulled out a scroll with a sigil on it and set about casting it.

However, the sigil came to life as soon as he opened the scroll, and a sword sliced through Seneschal, as two angels emerged and flew by my side.

One of them I recognized as an emaciated Gabriel, weak and barely able to stand.

Holding him up was Jehudiel, sword in hand.

"My apologies," he said. "Did we interrupt your plans?"

30

Jehudiel swung at Greede. His sword cleft through the latter's thick arm, severing it. The impact of the blow also sent Greede flying backwards.

Meanwhile I was left holding Gabriel. It was like grasping a skeleton. His bones were visible beneath papery white skin, his golden hair mattered and patchy, his golden eyes broken, sunken, and his breathing ragged.

But I could still feel his power. There was a supernova burning inside of him, weak but present. Greede hadn't managed to kill him totally, and I understood why Jehudiel had risked so much to get him back.

Gabriel was the Virtue that countered Sloth. He was our only shot at balancing out the scales and defeating Greede.

Jehudiel once again stood next to me. Anael followed suit.

"You know what must be done," he told her.

A tear streaked down her face, but she said nothing. I had witnessed that silence before—the silence of a soldier.

Jehudiel knelt by Gabriel and took his hands.

"What are you doing?" I asked.

Jehudiel gave me a solemn look. "I am giving this soul life."

It dawned on me.

"You're giving him your grace."

Jehudiel did not answer. He needn't to. Placing a hand on the broken angel's chest, he began glowing softly.

"You're going to kill yourself so that he can live."

Again, he said nothing.

I wanted to say more. I wanted to tell him to stop. Jehudiel and I had known each other forever. He was the first archangel I had met, the first of that kind to consider me an equal, or at least someone not to be brushed off.

He had shared his magic with me.

But I couldn't say anything. He was doing the right thing, for all of us. This one act could end up saving the whole universe. I wanted to stop him. He was my friend, he was my ally. He was *there* and that is what friends do.

So instead I nodded at him and said,

"Thank you."

He smiled. "You are most welcome, my friend."

His wings withered and fell, and with those final words, Jehudiel, Virtue of Chastity, friend of humanity, expired.

His grace—a ball of light so bright that it felt like a miniature sun—sunk into Gabriel's chest, and ignited.

The angel sat up, eyes wide open. His wings flared. He found his feet and then took to the air, hovering off the ground, arms spread, wings stretched, hair billowing. Heat emanated from him, pushing back against the frigid Antarctic climate.

He reminded me of that emaciated Superman from the *Flashpoint Paradox*. All thin and wiry, and then he gets exposed to the sun and utterly annihilates everyone in front of him. Gabriel was the same. One minute he was on the brink of death, the next he was a living cosmic god, rivaling the actual gods who were still watching us from the sidelines and refusing to lift a finger.

Screw them, we could take care of our own problems.

Greede brushed snow and dirt off his shoulders.

"So," he sneered. "You survive. Yet again."

"Alan Greede," Gabriel said. The ground trembled at the sound of his voice. "You shall pay for your sins."

The angel shot forwards, a broadsword in hand, and slashed at Greede. The latter ducked, threw a bolt of fiery magic at him, and rebounded for another attack...

A luminous spear impaled his leg from behind. Greg snarled, his mouth bloody.

"Forgot about us?"

Luke burst from the ground. His whole body was glowing like hot coals. Twin lasers—narrow focused beams of fire and heat—shot from his hands, searing into Greede.

Seneschal leapt into action—and was immediately pounced upon by a feral Morgana, who swore in wild Celtic while tearing at him with her swords. Niamh stood just far enough to make her spear useful, and the two Fey practically shredded the Slime.

"You traitorous snot-ball," cried Mustafa. He clapped his hands together. Invisible energy collated around Seneschal, trapping him in an orb. The orb began shrinking. Seneschal's body twisted and spiked, fighting back against the barrier, but Mustafa, bloody and sweating, with veins popping out of his neck and forehead, held on.

Evans hobbled up to the barrier. One of his arms was missing, revealing a clay-brown stump beneath. He wrapped his other, massive arm around the barrier, and yellow-green sigils glowed all over his body. Electricity bounced around inside the barrier, cooking Seneschal alive. The Slime's translucent body clumped up and became a syrupy mess, like burnt caramel.

Mustafa yelled in effort and slapped his hands closed, and the barrier imploded with a disgusting squelching sound, and when the barrier was released, the Slime was no more, leaving behind a puddle of opaque water. Morgana spat on it.

Meanwhile, Gabriel, Luke, and Greg were holding back Greede but the latter was fighting back. I raised my sword to go help them.

"No," Anael said. She held out an arm to hold me back. "It is too late."

"Are you kidding? This is our chance."

She shook her head. "No. It comes."

We all felt the presence.

It started with the temperature. The cold in Antarctica is omni-present. It is just as relevant as any person you are with. It requires attention and care, and one mistake will cost you your life. So you adopt it into your routine. We hadn't been there long enough for that, so we felt it in our bones.

So when things got warm, we noticed. And I'm not talking Bahamas warm. This was volcano-warm.

Hell-warm.

The air thickened, forming a massive heat haze that fell from the sky. It didn't have an end—it was as if the sky had decided to bulk up and fall down on us.

A few feet from us, light began to gather. There was a terrible pressure, like atmospheric pressure, except there was nothing gradual about this. At first I thought it was a summoning, but the lack of Anima Particles—little bits of living magic that slip past the spell—suggested that whatever was coming through had not bothered with an invitation.

It just kicked the door down and waltzed right in.

From a sphere of fire and light emerged lances of light. Twelve of them in total. The sphere was easily twelve feet tall. It cracked like an eggshell and flames burst forth.

Hellfire.

It was every color and smell but there's a reason why brimstone is often mentioned. It's because it leaves an impression. Brimstone smells of death and decay. Whatever was coming through was coated in it.

A pair of clawed human hands pushed the crack open, and through it, a man walked.

A man made out of Hellfire, a swirling mass of roaring, stinking, yellow, red and black flames, in the shape of a man. The cocoon melted away, but the twelve wings attached themselves to the back of this creature and gave it a more three-dimensional shape.

Suddenly, my nightmare was in front of me again.

It was him, the creature who had killed me. Who had stopped my powers, thrown me off a helicopter and sent me to my death.

He was six feet of perfection, with beautiful alabaster skin, and long ebony hair that fell in perfect strands. He wore angelic armor that was blemished with fire stains, melted gold, and what looked like blood. His wings flared, their tips disappearing into the air around him, as if he was tapping into a world beyond our world.

Everything stopped. Everyone tensed.

Only Sun Tzu had the ability to speak.

"The Calamity."

31

He turned to Sun Tzu and the gods.

"Depart."

That one word had enough power to send me to my knees. I was not alone. Only Greede and the gods remained upright.

The gods stood there for a second. Then Zeus raised his hand. The Aegis shield flew from beneath the rubble to his hands, while Cernunnos summoned the Spear of the Sun back into his. Only the Sword of Michael remained there. The Calamity regarded it with sheer disgust and the fiery sword dulled.

This guy's *glower* could make the most holy of weapons shy away.

The gods turned and disappeared. Sun Tzu was the last to leave. He gave the Calamity a scowl that came with a roll of thunder but in the end, he too left.

Gabriel turned to face the new enemy. His broadsword was shaking so much he couldn't keep it still.

"We need to run," Anael said. "Gabriel."

"No!" He tried, and failed, to steady his sword. "I will not let Jehudiel's sacrifice be in vain."

Anael didn't give him a chance. She rushed him from behind, knocked him out with a backhanded strike and the two shot off into the sky.

The Calamity watched them with something akin to amusement. His smile was sinister and sagacious at the same time.

Then he looked at Greede and there was no more smiling.

"You."

Flames, magic, light, and dark raged around him. There was no telling what kind of magic this guy was using. There was no defining it. This guy was *power* itself, limitless and omnipotent.

So powerful he sent gods and angels running for the hills.

"Me," Greede said stepping up to him. He was grinning. "You came. And here I was, thinking that Azazel was too much of a coward to respond to my challenge. He does love hiding behind his favorite minion."

"Your words... they will get you killed. Slowly."

Greede shrugged casually. "The time for your threats is over."

"Indeed."

And the Calamity swung a fist upwards. Magic and fire swung from him, caught Greede under the chin and punted him twenty feet into the sky.

The Calamity looked at the rest of us. He didn't even speak, nor move. He didn't have to.

Flames rushed towards the Grigori before anyone could react. Luke held up his hands, thinking he could redirect the flames but this wasn't our magic. Those flames weren't normal flames and the result was him being jettisoned into a glacier with so much force that I heard bones snap.

The same spell pulverized Evans the golem as he shielded Greg. The Kresnik wasn't spared, either. His right side was crushed beneath force and fire, and when he fell to the ground he did not get up. On the other side, Morgana and Niamh screamed in agony as fire carpeted over them, and only a heavily injured Emrys—who had healed enough to call upon the Earth—saved them. There was a flash of light and when it was over, all three of them were on the ground. Emrys looked charred to a crisp. Mustafa screamed and then was cut off abruptly. I saw his arm flying in the air.

I watched all this a split-second before that magic hit me...

And passed by without so much as tussling my hair.

The Calamity now turned fully towards me as if seeing me for the first time.

"You are still alive. You live after I killed you."

The way he spoke made me think he hadn't used an actual physical language in quite a while (try, a few centuries), and more alarmingly, hadn't spoken to another being.

He couldn't. This was a creature so powerful it would atomize anything it came in contact with.

"Yeah," I said, ignoring the tremble in my voice. "You threw me off the chopper. You blocked my powers and killed me."

"Your powers?" He cocked his head. Beautify ebony hair swayed hypnotically. "Ah, I see. You believe you have power. Magic, you call it."

He raised a hand and his magic coalesced into a fireball that let out a whining roar.

"Your power is akin to dust," he said. "*This* is true power. Now expire along with the rest of your species."

He threw the fireball in my direction. It was too fast to dodge, too big to block, too intense to take. All I could do was brace myself for impact.

It never came—because I was saved by the last creature I thought would come to my aid.

The fireball evaporated. A hobbled, cloaked creature stood just inches away from my feet, one gnarled arm extended. For the first time, I saw his skin—it was grey-blue with specks of light, making it look like a starry night sky.

Azazel looked at me, one silvery eye visible beneath the obfuscation of the cloak, and my shadows went crazy.

I had no control. It was an automatic response, just like adrenaline. Shadows erupted from me, coating me in black armor and magic, while Djinn sang with power.

Azazel chuckled.

"You grow stronger, Erik Ashendale," he said in his usual raspy voice. He turned to address his myrmidon. "This creature is paramount to my end goal. You will not destroy it. Not yet."

He pointed ahead. "*That,* however, is to be annihilated."

Greede snarled and raised his arms. Boulders of ice and rock flew towards the Calamity like meteorites. The latter stood there while the projectiles vaporized before they touched him.

"You showed up!" Greede cried, pointing at me. "For *him!*"

Azazel let out a low growl. "You have three of my Sins, mortal pest. You will return them."

In response, Greede raised his hands and black lightning fell from the sky. The necromantic spell turned anything it touched into a pool of decayed matter. The Calamity raised his hand and fire shielded him, albeit the spell ate through the flames.

Black lightning also rained on Azazel who looked at me and said,

"Protect me."

Suddenly I was shielding the little creature, shadows raised into a shield of black that ate up the necromantic spell. With a cry I willed myself away.

"What the fuck did you do to me?" I cried.

Azazel chuckled.

"Oh, you don't know yet," he taunted. "That power you have, it is not human, Erik Ashendale. It is something far, far older than you think. Older than angels and demons. Older than Heaven and Hell. It is a power only I can remember."

I opened my mouth to speak but he said "Quiet."

My mouth was clamped shut. I grit my teeth instead and raised my sword... or I would have, were it not for my magic working against me.

In a fit of desperation, I willed my shadows away, and suddenly I was free. An instant later, the Calamity struck me and down I went. He kicked me away and I felt my chest caving in. Healing magic went crazy trying to save my lungs from collapsing.

"Stay down there, Erik Ashendale," Azazel said. "And watch what happens to those who defy me." He nodded at the Calamity. "You may use it. And once you do, this world is yours to take. Have fun."

And just like that he disappeared into thin air.

The Calamity threw his head back and laughed. How could something so melodious and beautiful come from such an evil being?

Greede cracked his neck. "You have not won yet, Pride."

"Pride?" The Calamity cocked his head in amusement. "I have not begun using my Sin yet." His grin was enough to send me screaming—if I had any breath left. "I want to play with you, mortal. Amuse me."

And then Greede proceeded to pull off some truly incredible feats of magic.

First, a wall of sigils appeared behind him, each raining down lasers and fire bolts. Lightning fell from the sky. All the while, Greede ran around, placing sigils on the ground that glowed purple.

The Calamity effortlessly dodged and blocked, never attacking, always redirecting.

Greede spread his arms and time stopped.

Not metaphorically.

His monstrous form sweated from using one of the most complex branches of magic ever: time manipulation.

The Calamity froze in place. He began moving in slow, slugging ways, while Greede rushed him. Spikes of ice, lances of earth and rock, fire and lightning bolts, as well as punches from Greede's thick arms, landed on the Calamity without the latter having a chance to block.

Clones of Greede popped out, adding to the melee, while the real Greede ran towards a crater in the ground. The same spot where Zeus and Cernunnos had retrieved their weapons from.

Greede was going for the Sword of Michael.

The Necronomicon appeared in his hands, and he grasped the Sword. He screamed when the holy weapon touched a guy with not so holy powers, but it was absorbed by the power of Gluttony and the Necronomicon.

"NO!"

The Calamity shattered the time spell with just one syllable. Greede turned, and the air around him became filled with multiple copies of the Sword of Michael, all flaming and posed to shoot themselves like arrows towards the Calamity.

Greede yelled a war cry. The swords fired. They hit the Calamity, going past his flames and through his armor, and drawing lava-like blood.

For the first time, he screamed in agony. Bits of his flesh turned necrotic and fell off. The Sword of Michael was very much anti-Calamity.

"How does it feel?" Greede roared over the sound of magic and agony. "How does it feel to experience pain? To be the victim instead of the abuser? How does it feel, Prince of Lies, to be weak?"

The Calamity dodged a blade and summoned his own flaming sword. His was black-flamed.

Greede summoned a large two-handed version of the Sword of Michael, and the two clashed. Greede, who had never been much of a fencer, cheated. He sprung another pair of arms—with another sword—and impaled the Calamity, then kicked him away.

The Calamity landed on ice and stayed down.

"You cannot beat me now, Pride," said Greede, walking up to him. "You cannot defeat me. You are just one Sin; I am three. Soon to be four."

He reached the Calamity.

And then... FIRE.

Not just heat. Fire. Pure, unleashed, uncontrolled fire.

Fire so hot it evaporated the ice in goddamn *Antarctica*!

The ground shook as tons of ice disappeared, leaving behind black rock that was scorched. Behind us, glaciers cracked and parted. Water rose to meet the ice. Steam hissed violently as cold and hot battled one another.

Behind Greede, the Calamity appeared. He was transformed into a humanoid with no features, a creature made out of lava, light, and fire. Horns jutted out from his head, a forked tail swished behind, and cloven hooves replaced its feet. Its twelve wings blackened before I realized they had turned so bright that all I could make out was a dark outline.

The image was familiar iconography. Go to any museum and you'll see him on a dozen paintings, immortalizing the embodiment of what the Church tells us evil should look like:

The horns, the hooves, the twelve wings, the evil angel vibe, the Prince of Lies, the Sin of Pride.

Lucifer—the first archangel, the Light-Bearer of God, the Beast, the Devil, Satan himself—raised his right hand. Light formed a thin shaft that ended in a double-headed axe that curved wildly.

He raised the weapon and, in a voice dripping with all the evil in the world, said,

"One is all I need."

He swung the axe down upon Greede. The force of the blow not only cleft through demonic flesh and bone but bore a fissure in the ground so deep I could not see the bottom. All I know is that the ground began shaking in an earthquake that threatened to split the world's largest continent to pieces.

All from one swing.

From what was left of Greede's husk, I saw a figure jettison out. The Necronomicon flashed black against the icy landscape, and there was a pop of magic.

Greede had escaped again, taking with him the Sword of

Michael, and leaving behind the literal Devil in a very irate mood.

I was screwed.

Beyond screwed.

I was...

There are no words. I am powerful, but not this level of powerful. I mean, there is punching above your weight-class, and then there is a literal galaxy's worth of power coming at you with an axe.

Only Lucifer never did.

He looked at the spot Greede had escaped from and sighed. Then he turned his fiery gaze at me.

"It begins."

And he took off like a rocket and disappeared into the sky.

BEFORE I COULD BLINK, the ground beneath me groaned in protest. Ice cracked and exploded. I slipped and threw myself aside to avoid being swallowed by ice.

The Grigori were not so lucky. Those still alive cried out but there was no one to help them.

No one to help us.

It didn't matter that Lucifer had left me alive. There was no way out of here.

Suddenly, globules of white mist appeared seemingly at random but I could tell they were in the places where the Grigori had been. Pops of magic went off in sequence, and the wind picked up behind me.

Mephisto emerged from a portal, snatched the back of my coat, and hauled me through a portal just as the ground I was standing on became swallowed by a tsunami of Antarctic water.

32

I tumbled down a set of stairs and came to a halt in front of Abi. She helped me up and squeezed my ribs with enough resolve to crush them again.

"Easy, easy," I said. "What's going on?"

All around us, the mansion was in full assault mode. From outside I could see—and hear—the full-scale war going on.

"Erik!"

My sister appeared by my side and once again my ribs ached.

"Gil," I said. "When did you get back?" Then I remembered the globes of white light that appeared over the Grigori. "Was that you back then? Did you rescue us?"

She nodded. "As soon as Michael dumped me back in here." There was a maniacal glint in her eyes. "I have so much to tell you."

"Where are they? Are they still alive?"

The two women fell silent.

"Tell me," I said.

"Evans is out of it," Abi said. "The backlash from the

golem fried his brain for a while. He's hooked up to IVs and life support. Greg needs two surgeries and several pins in his arm and leg. Luke... his spine is broken. Doctors say he will be wheelchair-bound for the rest of his life."

Cold that had nothing to do with the Antarctic washed over me.

"Mustafa is dead," Abi went on. Her tone was neutral, calm and efficient. Detached. "He bled out from a torn arm. Emrys is in a coma. We think it's self-induced but there is very little we know about Druid techniques, so we don't know when, if ever, he'll wake up."

"Master Gil!"

Mephisto ran towards Gil.

"More are coming. I have a report from the front lines."

Gil nodded. She looked at me.

"Whatever that thing was that attacked you," she said, "it unleashed an army on Earth. Come."

I thought we were heading for the war room, but instead, Gil went into an elevator and pressed a button. We started going up.

"Asmodaii appeared en masse," she said. "My sources tell me that Eureka was hit the hardest but several legions have emerged in every major city. We think they are following ley lines, but again, there are so many of them and they spread fast. I have strike teams deployed." She turned and offered me a smile that never reached her eyes.

"But not in this town. We have our own guardian here who single-handedly started tearing them apart."

"Who?" I asked.

"See for yourself."

The elevator dinged. We were on the roof and I walked towards the edge.

It was like a landscape shot in a zombie apocalypse movie.

Beyond the forest tree line, where the city began, smoke plumed. Cars crashed. Buildings shook and fell. The screams of people carried in the winds.

All around Asmodaii emerged.

Tall, lanky creatures with chitinous armor and blank faces, they were Hell's shock troops. On their reverse-jointed legs they could cover incredible distances, and most of them had curved claws long enough to qualify as swords, in lieu of hands.

I had faced them before. They were bad news in the worst possible way.

But they were being beaten.

A blur of dust and rock barreled through their ranks, leaving behind gore and guts, and a squishing noise that followed, like the sonic boom of an aircraft that had already taken off. One of the showers was too close to the mansion, and while the barriers fended off unwanted attacks, there was nothing there to stop bloody showers.

Guess Gil hasn't spent as much time around my familiar as I have.

Amaymon took to the air and landed like a cat, poised and balanced, and utterly covered in Asmodaii guts. His shape was human, but his hands ended in wicked claws and his eyes were wide and feral. He kept the cat ears too, as well as two ebony tails that swished like lashes behind him.

He made a beeline for me and there was a split second where I thought he was going to kill me. Such was his intensity. However, the demon stopped inches from my face and grinned.

"You missed me."

"I thought you were dead."

"You thought a couple of angels are enough to keep me down?"

"You were in a coma. In a tank."

"I was gettin' some beauty sleep for the party."

"Only you would be happy with a full-scale demonic invasion."

He chuckled. "I sensed the bad guy. He's strong."

"He is. He's the devil. Lucifer. Sin of Pride."

"Shit. Why do you always get to meet the celebrities first?"

"Next time I'll make sure to get you an autograph."

"All I ask."

I reached out and we traded grips.

"Glad you're fine, buddy."

He nodded.

"Brother," Mephisto said. "Status report."

"Well, if you got off your ass and came down to help, you'd know the goddamn status yourself."

"I was retrieving your mortal partner from certain death."

"Yeah, I gotta give him that one," I said. "Though next time make less with the yanking and more with the 'come with me if you want to live.' Way better response."

"Amaymon," Gil said, walking towards the edge. We joined her. "How bad is it?"

He needn't answer. We knew. We could feel it deep in our stomachs. People always can, even if they don't practice magic. We might have lost touch with our spiritual nature but that didn't mean we had forgotten about it.

Or that it had forgotten about us.

We were symbiotic with our world, and our world was crying in agony at this moment.

"It's the goddamn apocalypse," he answered. "Asmodaii keep on coming. Hell's gates have been flung wide open."

There was a moment where we all held our breaths, forced ourselves to swallow, and tried not freak out.

I remembered Azazel's parting words to Lucifer:

This world is yours to take.

The Devil had been unleashed upon us. It was a literal Hell on Earth.

And we were the only ones who stood in their way.

***

*Erik Ashendale returns in **FALLEN** - All-out war has hit Eureka! With a full scale invasion, a demon strong enough to kill archangels, and the army shooting at anything that moves, no corner is safe.*

Peace is a thing of the past — It's a good thing he's ready for war...

> Get **Fallen - The Warlock Legacy Book 10**,
> Or turn the page for a preview!

***

FALLEN - PREVIEW

It's hard to get french fries during the apocalypse.

"I thought we were going to Wendy's," Abi whispered hoarsely as we took refuge inside what had been a thriving fast-food joint just a week ago. Now the world had collectively learnt to stay indoors and barricade against the demons steadily pouring in.

I shrugged. "There's no line here."

She raised her eyebrows. "There's also no electricity, no employees, the food is starting to turn, and I think the back of the building is gone."

"Yeah." I grinned. "But *no line*."

We weren't here for food. My sister has a mansion stocked with enough grub to feed an army.

Literally, since she has her own army.

No, Abi and I were here because this place was a checkpoint and who doesn't like a french fry break? Outside, I could hear the growling and hissing of demonic invaders, coupled with the staccato of gunfire and occasional scream as weak human flesh met demonic teeth and talons. Human law enforcement had tried handling it at first and failed miserably. Now everywhere you walked the streets were slick with blood, leaving a metallic taste in your mouth. There was the stench of gore in the air like a butcher shop, only the demons made no effort to hide the carcasses.

The apocalypse had started less than two weeks ago when the topmost supernatural forces on planet Earth, and myself, were sent on a mission to the South Pole in order to prevent the awakening of a very powerful demon.

We were backstabbed and failed. But the bad guys' real goal wasn't just awakening the Sin of Sloth. That had been the opening act, the shitty band you have to power through before you get to the good stuff.

The last of the Seven Deadly Sins came into play. You might have heard of him, he's the literal Devil, and he decided to turn Earth into a wasteland. Exactly five minutes later the first Asmodaii, Hell's shock troops, were deployed on Earth and it's been a nightmare ever since.

Places like where I live, the La Fortunata district of Eureka, were hit especially hard. We are a focal point of magic due to a high concentration of supernatural anomalies over the decades. The magic in the city attracted demons like cow dung attracts flies, and when Lucifer opened the floodgates, there was no warning.

Thousands perished on day one. For our own sanity we stopped counting after that.

Abi shook her head, red hair tied back in a ponytail that whipped about with the motion, and was about to say something in response to my misanthropy, when we heard something crash from the back of the building where the Drive Thru window had once been.

I wordlessly cocked my head, signaling I would go first. This was supposed to be a stealth mission. Go in, find the

Wound, seal it up and get out without losing too many people.

See, demons can't just pop into our existence without help. There are some very strong barriers in place in order to keep our dimensions separate. So you get portals in one of two ways:

The first is magic users. Most Adepts aren't strong enough to open a portal big enough for an imp, let alone a full-grown Asmodaii. Granted, the current situation saturated Earth's ambient magic to the point where even weak practitioners got themselves a solid boost. Wizards and Witches, the level after Adept, can manage portals. I've never dabbled much in them—I get motion sickness—but it's not unheard of. Specialists rarely specialized in portals. Warlocks like my sister could—it had been their bread and butter once upon a time—but those days are long gone and if they open portals, they do so with loads of preempted calculations and care.

The second way you can get portals like this is by being a creature so metaphysically large, you start ripping the very fabric of reality. That was Lucifer for us. With each passing second he was tearing more and more seams into our reality, through which Asmodaii kept pouring.

Something bumped into the kitchen counter and as I shuffled closer I could see the Asmodaii's head.

These demons were tall and lanky, built like taut strings, all gangly arms which ended with an oversized forward-curved talon that brought to mind images of scythes and sickles. Its face was a round bulbous thing, with a face plate that denied it any expression or even orifices. The Asmodaii was milky white and grey, with patches of black and brown, one of which occupied its face plate. There were no eyes or ears, no mouth, nothing with which to breathe because it didn't need to.

The Asmodaii made a series of clicking sounds, echolocation maybe, we hadn't figured it out yet, and shuddered when the sounds bounced off the reflective metallic surfaces of the kitchen. One of its clawed spindly legs stepped on a frying pan and pressed down with enough force to perforate the iron.

It came closer.

I saw Abi raise her weapon, an M4 carbine, and assume a kneeling firing stance. Her lips were tight and formed a slight opening for her to exhale as she settled into the shot. Her finger was already curled around the trigger. I tapped her lightly on the shoulder and shook my head. The shot would attract others and then our position would be compromised.

She lowered the weapon and grimaced. I pointed at a rack of knives, spoons and ladles on the wall. She looked up at me quizzically. I grinned. She rolled her eyes and focused her vision on the rack. She kept her magic condensed, given that Asmodaii could sense power. This one clicked excitedly when it felt Abi's magic.

Suddenly the rack toppled over, sending metal utensils spinning in the air and clattering loudly on the ground. The Asmodaii turned.

I struck.

Unlike other magic users, I had once had a curse which looped my magic inside my body. This had meant I could not cast spells, but could heal almost instantly from anything and empower my body to superhuman levels. Since then I had regained my magic but I had never had any trouble with moving large amounts of power in the first place.

My stride covered far more ground than any regular human, and as the Asmodaii's head was turned, I caught it completely unaware. My magical shortsword, Djinn, was already in my hands, tip down, and I buried it with all my strength inside the demon's neck, right at the base of the spine.

Asmodaii are tough. You can't just stab them like that. Even with my enchanted muscles I had to wrap my arm around the demon's neck and lever the sword deeper. The demon struggled and whipped its arms around. Talons ripped deep grooves into silvery aluminum surfaces. I twisted and pushed, and the demon's head fell over with a squelching sound. Black ichor spilled down my front, ruining yet another outfit. At this rate I was going to run out of clothes by the end of the week.

If we survive this, I'm sending Hell my dry-cleaning bill.

The Asmodaii stumbled but wasn't down just yet. We'd had multiple reports that this new batch could operate for a few minutes with their heads cut off, or holes blown up in their torsos from grenades and high-powered munitions.

I stabbed the demon in its belly, sword sinking in easier this time, and channeled just enough magic to blast an energy beam from each of its edges, one up, one down. The result was a thin pane of azure-colored laser that cut the demon neatly in half as if I had taken a buzzsaw to it.

Beheaded and bifurcated the demon still swung its arms impotently from the ground before more ichor spilled and it finally died out. I released a sigh of relief and chuckled, when suddenly the front doors of the restaurant burst open and a bloodied black cop threw himself in. A pair of Asmodaii leapt after him. One of them raised a talon. The cop screamed. He raised his baton which had already saved him at least once judging from the damage on it.

"Shit," I swore.

Abi and I both reacted at the same time. Her M4 barked as a three-round burst smacked into the attacking Asmodaii's face plate. Her grouping was excellent.

I was less subtle.

An energy streak shot from Djinn and caught both demons, pulverizing the injured Asmodaii's head while throwing the other one back outside and slamming into a Fiat hard enough to fold it over.

The cop looked up at us. Abi offered him a hand.

"Who are you people?" he demanded, glaring at my sword and black coat.

Before I could answer, the Asmodaii outside leapt out of the wreckage and emitted a shriek—one that was answered by a chorus of clicks and chirps, followed by a torrent of the eerie clicking of spindly legs against asphalt as dozens of the demon's brothers answered its call.

So much for stealth.

Abi grabbed the cop and dragged him back into the kitchen. As she went, she ripped one of the several grenades from her vest, pulled the pin, and threw it. It exploded in the distance, and I heard one of the Asmodaii cry out.

"Code four," I heard Abi cry into her earpiece. "Code four. It's been Eriked."

"What?" I asked, hearing my name. "What's Eriked?"

"Sorry, sir," came the captain's voice from my earpiece. "We have our own version of FUBAR."

"My name means FUBAR?" I asked incredulously. "Whose idea was this? Was it Gil's?"

"It was mine," Abi said with a grin.

"You're my girlfriend!"

"Which gives me the right to name things after you. It's romantic."

"We are so having a talk after this."

"Who the hell are you people?" cried the cop again. "What the fuck is that?"

We went past the dead Asmodaii in the kitchen and kept going until we stepped over the hole in the wall. The sun beamed down on us as we strode into the parking lot.

"Hell, might not be the word you want to use right now," I said as we stopped.

We had to.

The parking lot was littered with demons, each one a killing machine targeting us.

Abi raised her rifle, a grim expression on her face. "Captain," she hissed into the earpiece, "we need reinforcements. About right the fuck now."

"On your ten, inbound in two minutes."

"We don't have two minutes."

I stepped forward holding up my sword and poured magic into it.

"We do."

This time I did not hold back. That same curse that runs in my family had also endowed me with an extraordinary amount of magic. Power cascaded around me, flowing through the sword. Its blade flared blue as energy piled around it, forming a massive blade three times its original size. Arcs of azure lightning leapt out. Shadows drew around my body, and the air around me grew thick with static and raw untapped magic.

The Asmodaii instinctively stepped back.

"Get ready," I said. "I'm gonna Erik this up big time."

***

Get Fallen - The Warlock Legacy Book 10 today!

FREE NOVELLA

Get a FREE prequel story
Wolf's Bane - The Warlock Legacy #0
as well as private giveaways, early access to future books, and MORE!

Click the image or visit http://eepurl.com/bkDPGr

BEFORE YOU GO…

This is the part where I kindly ask you to leave a review for *Shattered*. Reviews are hugely important for authors because we depend on word-of-mouth and enthusiasm from readers like you.

So please help spread the word and leave a review!

Thanks! :)

ABOUT THE AUTHOR

Ryan Attard is the author of the Warlock Legacy series and a host of other fantasy works.

Hailing from a faraway island, it was only a matter of time before he began creating imaginary friends and writing down their adventures.

Nowadays you can find him toiling over his next project, rolling dice in D&D campaigns, looking up stuff online that surely garnered the attention of the authorities, and cackling when his fans shake their fists angrily at him for playing with their heart strings.

He also enjoys writing about himself in the third person. Say hi on Facebook, Instagram, or email at ryanattardauthor@gmail.com

THE WARLOCK LEGACY

DO YOU HAVE THE ENTIRE *WARLOCK LEGACY* SERIES?

Firstborn
Birthright
Lost Ones
Judgement
Nemesis
Resurrection
Broken
Blood Rites
Shattered
Fallen

Click HERE to check out the whole series!

Or here to get the BOX SET (at a discount)!!

Printed in Great Britain
by Amazon